THE GROANING GALLOWS

The Stories of Murders and of Men and Women who faced the Executioner in York, E. Yorks and N. Lincs.

by

A. A. CLARKE

ARTON BOOKS 1994

Published by Arton Books
P. O. Box 5, Hornsea, North Humberside, HU18 1US

Copyright © 1994 by A. A. Clarke

All rights reserved. No part of this publication may be reproduced or transmitted in any form or by any means, electronic or mechanical, including photocopying, recording or any information storage and retrieval system, without permission in writing from the publishers, Arton Books, P. O. Box 5, Hornsea, North Humberside, HU18 1US

*Printed by Clifford Ward & Co.
(Bridlington) Ltd.,
55 West Street, Bridlington, East Yorkshire
YO15 3DZ*

ISBN 0 9522163 5 3

ACKNOWLEDGEMENT

I wish to express my deepest gratitude to the Humberside County Archivist, the Local Studies Librarian in Hull, and Libraries of York and Lincoln and their staff for unfailing assistance and courtesy during my researches. In particular I would like to thank the staff at Record Management Services, Home Office with whose help, cases where publication and scrutiny had been banned, were made subject to accelerated opening for me.

Ordnance Survey maps are reproduced by permission of The Controller, Ordnance Survey, Southampton.

Extracts from the *Hull Daily Mail* are reproduced by kind permission of that newspaper.

CONTENTS

		Page
(1)	Introduction	7
(2)	Tragedy at Owthorne	17
(3)	Dick Turpin — Highwayman & Murderer	22
(4)	Black Deeds at Beningbrough Hall	30
(5)	Murder at Leconfield	35
(6)	Jealousy at the Farm	43
(7)	Cheating the Hangman in Beverley	51
(8)	Cruel Murder in Hull's Fishing Fleet	54
(9)	The Deeming Case	58
(10)	A Champion Murderer	61
(11)	Heartless Crime in Hull	67
(12)	The Sleeping Murderer	75
(13)	Murder at Scampston	79
(14)	Black Tuesdays	83
(15)	Death on a Withernsea Beach	89
(16)	The Molescroft Murder	91
(17)	A Drummer Boy's Escape from the Hangman	96
(18)	The Lincolnshire Murderess	104
(19)	Son of a Police Inspector	108
(20)	The Man Who Wanted to Hang	112
(21)	Murder in York	118
(22)	Murder in the Desert	121
(23)	Eternal Triangle at Hessle	124
	Epilogue	126

AUTHOR'S NOTE

All the incidents in the book are based on recorded facts. However material facts on some of them, particularly the earlier ones, are scarce. To ensure a readable narrative I have used a modicum of licence to overcome this.

Society in Victorian England while considered prudish in the extreme was in fact readily willing to be regaled with salacious facts of cases, particularly murders. Some of the reporting went beyond the bounds of what would be considered decent today but I have nevertheless related the facts as printed in press reports of the day. Those in the Stoner case are unfortunately particularly ghoulish.

"The world itself is just a large prison, out of which some are daily lead to execution" – Sir Walter Raleigh

THE GROANING GALLOWS
Introduction

Society has always had problems finding suitable forms of punishment for those committing crimes. Earliest punishment took three simple forms, banishment, execution and physical punishment.

Whipping was very common as a punishment at the end of the eighteenth and beginning of the nineteenth centuries, sometimes the sentence being carried out in private and, where an example was required, in public. In 1819 three boys were whipped in the yard of the Hull Gas Company for stealing food from a local baker by false pretences. In October the same year William Randerson was found guilty of stealing four stone of rope from Richard Dunn. He was tied to the tail of a cart and publicly flogged from Whitefriargate to the Old Dock Gate and back again. Still not appeased, the Authorities then sent him to the town gaol for three months hard labour. Lesser offences were often punished by periods of public humiliation in stocks or pillories.

Earliest confinement in prison was not used as punishment but simply as a place to hold those awaiting other sentences. The earliest gaol recorded in the town of Hull was in the Market Place at the corner of Butchery (now part of Queen Street and Myton Gate). The building was a four-storey block attached to the Guildhall and sometimes referred to as the Guildhall Tower. The lower floor was a damp single room dungeon, above was a floor for debtors and the top two floors held felons. There was no courtyard or other space for outside exercise, no sewer and no access to water. The gaolor lived in an adjoining house. In 1679 a chimney was constructed to allow fires to be lit in the coldest of weather.

The eighteenth century saw the start of custodial sentences and the building of a replacement prison in Castle Street was entrusted to local builders Edward and Thomas Riddle and opened in 1785 with the old building being demolished some seven years afterwards.

Beverley Sessions House where justice has been dispensed for nearly 200 years.

A 19th century miscreant placed in stocks.

Hull's oldest recorded gaol.

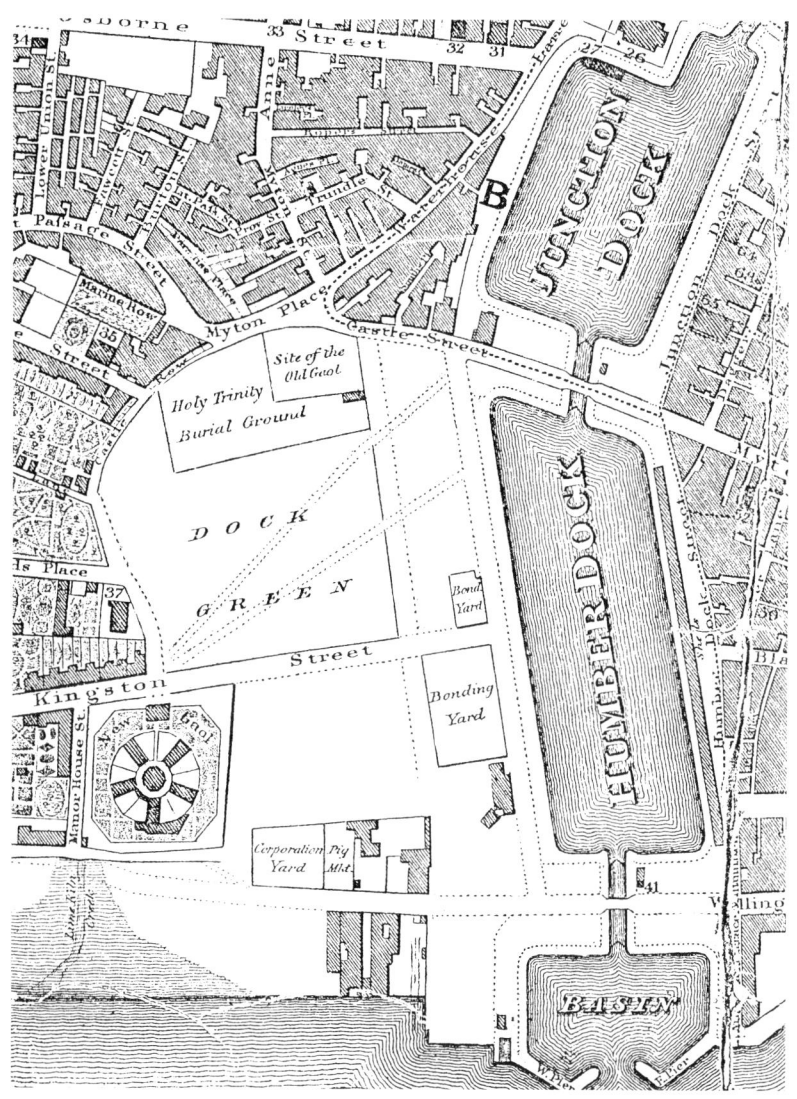

Showing five wing prison in Kingston Street, Hull and site of previous gaol.

Oblong in shape the new building had six large rooms, one attic and thirteen small rooms or cells as they were known. Also in the town was a small house of correction in Fetter Lane for receiving debtors and persons who had committed misdemeanours. In the 1830s Fetter Lane was to become the first headquarters for Hull's fledgling modern police force.

The Gaol Act of 1823 required all towns to have a better prison and in 1829 a five-wing building was opened in Kingston Street, Hull, based on the design of Pentonville Gaol in London with each wing radiating from a central hub as in some modern prisons. Only forty years afterwards the foundation stone was laid for the present day prison in Hedon Road.

An idea of the sort of sentences handed down by the East Riding County Quarter Sessions at the end of the 18th and beginning of the 19th Century can be gathered from the following cases:

20-year old Annette Ward sentenced at York Assizes to 2 months hard labour in 1892 for burglary at house of Thomas Sturdy in Market Weighton.

1740 Robert Briscoe of Burstwick — Stealing two rings — Transported for seven years!
1743 Margaret Boulton of Yapham — Stealing clothes — Publicly whipped through Pocklington.
1745 Benjamin Ackers of Wharram — Stealing linen — Publicly whipped in the Market Place.
1807 Joshua Ashton of Patrington — Stealing bacon and a handkerchief — Pressed to serve on H.M. Ships.
1812 Thomas Ash of Walkington — Stealing nine ducks — Transported for seven years.
1862 Mary Smith — Petty Larceny — Six years Penal Servitude.

The death sentence, that ultimate punishment, was originally carried out in public. These public spectacles were abolished in 1868 and the last public execution in Hull was that of John Rogerson who was hanged in 1778 on the gallows at the corner of

Great Thornton Street and Waverley Street. Gallows Lane ran from Pinfold Street to Anlaby Road. Old execution sites abound and their whereabouts are often denoted by names passed down through the ages. Gallows Hill remains at Skidby as does Gallows Field off Station Road in Howden. Beverley has its Gallows Lane just outside the North Bar.

John Rogerson had been convicted of forging coins in Hull and sentenced to death. He was incarcerated in the dungeon at the Guildhall prison to await his execution where the Reverend George Lambert of Fish Street Congregational Church found him in penitent mood. Days passed and when at last the fateful moment arrived and the door of the dungeon was opened, Rogerson walked calmly to the sledge waiting to convey him to the gallows already containing hs coffin. After mounting the gallows the rope was placed around his neck and he looked down and calmly addressed the large crowd gathered to witness his end. "Young people take warning. This is an affecting scene which is

27-year old Kate King sentenced to 3 months hard labour at York Assizes 1892 for stealing £8 at North Driffield.

Gallows Lane in Beverley.

now before you — a young man but 25 years of age about to be launched into eternity". With that the platform was drawn away and Rogerson died while members of the crowd either groaned or cried for mercy.

But while Hull and East Riding were dealing with some of their own cases most of the more serious matters, particularly those subject to the death penalty were heard at York Castle where the County Assize court for Yorkshire sat and where generations of locals from high born rebels to common thieves were judicially put to death and their bodies mutilated and publicly displayed as a deterrent to others.

York's famous and frequently used gallows were erected at Knavesmire about one mile south of the castle in 1379 by Joseph Penny a joiner of Blake Street at a cost of £10 15s. 0d. They replaced previous ones in the possession of the Abbot of St. Marys which were moved after disturbances by monks had taken place at one

John Rogerson rides in the sledge (two-wheeled) cart to "the fatal tree."

execution. In later years the military were to reoccupy York Castle and persons sentenced to death were returned to local gallows for execution.

The upper classes were virtually immune from justice for minor offences but high birth was no protection against the insatiable gallows. In August 1537 fifty-eight year old Sir Robert Aske and sixty-two year old Lord Hussey of Driffield were hanged for rebellion and after execution their bodies were taken to Master Robert Pyement's at the Eagle and Child for chains to be fitted on the remains. Next morning at 5.0 am the Sheriff and a troop of light horses took the bodies to a gibbet on Heworth Moor for public display.

In 1573, ten Yorkshire gentlemen including Robert de Schele, Edward de Lavoiffier and Robert de Alcock of Hull, Thomas de Berthollet from Driffield and William de Allembert from Pocklington were all executed for high treason. They were hanged and their bodies drawn and quartered. The mutilated limbs and severed heads were placed on gates and bars of York's walls.

Often the bodies of those executed were displayed at the places where the crime was committed as in the case of 34-years old William Penalton of Barmby who was executed in 1602 for the murder of John Young at Pocklington and whose body was hung in chains on Barmby Moor.

Occasionally executions were carried out with macabre results. On 27th May 1634 while Charles I ruled the country, John Bartendale, a young but hardened criminal, was executed at York for felony. After being allowed to hang for 45 minutes his body was cut down and buried near the place of execution outside Micklegate Bar. Shortly afterwards a Mr. Vavasour a gentleman from Hesslewood was riding by with his manservant when he thought he saw the earth move. Stopping, he ordered his servant to dismount and have a closer look. This worthy confirmed his suspicions and both men cleared some soil away and helped a bemused and shocked John Bartendale from his grave.

Re-imprisoned at the Castle by the astounded authorities he was taken before the same Judge who was so amazed at what appeared to be an act of Providence that he granted Bartendale a full pardon. Completely changed by his experience the young man became an honest hostler and was for ever a figure of some note in the city of York.

The forbidding doorway to York Castle.

It seems the hangmen in York were kept very busy, sometimes dealing with multiple executions to the great excitement of the ever present crowds of spectators.

On a cold and frosty 4th February 1634 ten men including thirty-four year old William Kitching of Little Driffield, were executed for rioting in Hull over corn and for demolishing the house of Edward Cooper, a corn merchant and stealing his clothing.

Religion and politics were both the cause of many executions and on 4th April 1649, the year Charles I was beheaded, fourteen men and seven women were executed for alleged rebellion. Thousands of spectators watched as they were taken in the carts to the gallows, holding each other's hands and quietly singing hymns. They included Henry Cave aged 39 and William Cropper, 40 years, both of Hull. All were remarkably assured and resigned to their fate and in five minutes 21 lifeless corpses were swinging "between earth and heaven — it was a most awful scene". On the same day Isabella Billington aged 32 was hung for the unbelievable crime of crucifying her mother and offering a calk and cock for a burnt sacrifice!

A century later in November 1746 ten more rebels, lead by Captain Hamilton were sentenced to death. One was reprieved on the way to the gallows and removed from the sledge. After hanging from the gallows for ten minutes the executioner cut down the bodies, laid them on the stage and stripped them naked. The Captain was the first to have his heart cut out and the executioner threw it on a fire crying, "Gentlemen, behold the heart of a traitor!" At this the crowd were reported to have given a loud huzza. The report continued by describing how the executioner then scored the arms and legs of the dead men without severing the limbs. He finished his work by chopping off each head. "Throughout, the whole proceedings was conducted with the utmost decency and good order!"

Highway robbery and the forging of money was common at the end of the eighteenth and beginning of the nineteenth centuries and perpetrators were shown no mercy by the Judges at York Assizes.

In 1804 Joseph Waller from Holme-on-Spalding Moor was executed for highway robbery at Gate Fulford. His victim had been a York Millwright, Thomas Potts. In 1824 William Potts held up the York to Hull coach at Pocklington and robbed the occupants. Within two months he had been arrested, tried and executed and his remains distributed among surgeons at Beverley and Hull for dissection!

Forgeries of coin of the realm was a real problem for the authorities and offenders seldom escaped with their lives. In 1810 Robert Vessey was executed for Uttering forged money at Seamer and Warter and the same year 38-years old Robert Burton and his wife Elizabeth, both living in Hull were executed for passing forged money to the Hull Bank of Peace, Harrison, Bedford and Waterton. In 1817 Samuel Leatherland was arrested for Possessing and Uttering forgeries in Hull and was executed the following year.

A few offenders were lucky — in 1787 John Plaxton of Beverley killed John Fenby, a miller. He appeared at York Assizes and was found guilty of Manslaughter and sentenced to a fine of one shilling and 21 days imprisonment. In 1813, William Ellis of Everingham was sentenced to death for stealing a horse from Matthew Ward. He was reprieved and the sentence commuted to 2 years imprisonment at Beverley.

There were still over 200 offences which carried the death penalty at the end of the 18th Century. gradually that number was reduced to a handful of crimes, but the ultimate offence in most people's minds — MURDER — continued to be a capital offence.

In 1957 Parliament, against the wishes of many people, restricted the death penalty to murders of a certain type. Murders of Police and Prison officers or murder "committed in the furtherance of theft" were the only ones where the death penalty remained. The law became ridiculous and dangerous. In 1965 the death penalty for murder was abolished completely and the only offences for which it now remains are Treason, Violent Piracy and, curiously, Arson in the Royal Dockyards.

The rest of this book tells the stories behind some of the people sentenced to death for murder in the area of Hull — York, the East Riding and North Lincolnshire.

TRAGEDY AT OWTHORNE

Generations of folk in Holderness, the flat and featureless south east corner of East Yorkshire, have fought a losing battle against the constantly raging north sea. Cliffs of clay are no protection from the pressures of the water and farm after farm, village after village have been swallowed up for ever with all traces of them washed away.

In the closing decades of the seventeenth century all that was left of the once proud village of Owthorne was a wild and desolate collection of five farms, a few cottages, a mill, a church and a vicarage. Already the wild north seas had ripped the muddy cliffs to within yards of the church chancel and not only were the living moving away but the dead were regularly washed away from the churchyard in churning seas.

The vicarage, itself only a short distance from the shore was home to the Reverend Enoch Sinclair, a devout and kindly bachelor whose household consisted of his two orphaned nieces Mary and Catherine and a cook, Mrs. Mott.

November 1683 saw particularly severe storms raging against north eastern coasts and wreckers were active in the Holderness area with false lights to lure unsuspectiong vessels to their doom. Whether as a result of this diabolical activity is not known but one dark night a three masted vessel foundered off the coast near Owthorne. Rallying a few of his strongest parishioners, among them William Dewlove, Henry Stephenson and the brothers Thomas and Abel Bird, the parson struggled to the shore to see if he could help any survivors. It was a macabre and eerie scene with crashing waves bringing flotsam ashore and more coffins from the cliffs above. But the parson and his friends were in search of life and sure enough, just as he was about to give up he heard a pathetic cry and found a sodden, half drowned human figure on the sand.

In the dim light he realised he was looking at a young woman and as she bent over her she pushed a tiny wet bundle into his arms, fell back and died. Looking into the sodden bundle Enoch saw a tiny baby which miraculously appeared to be still alive. Thrusting it to a woman who had accompanied them he told her to rush the child to

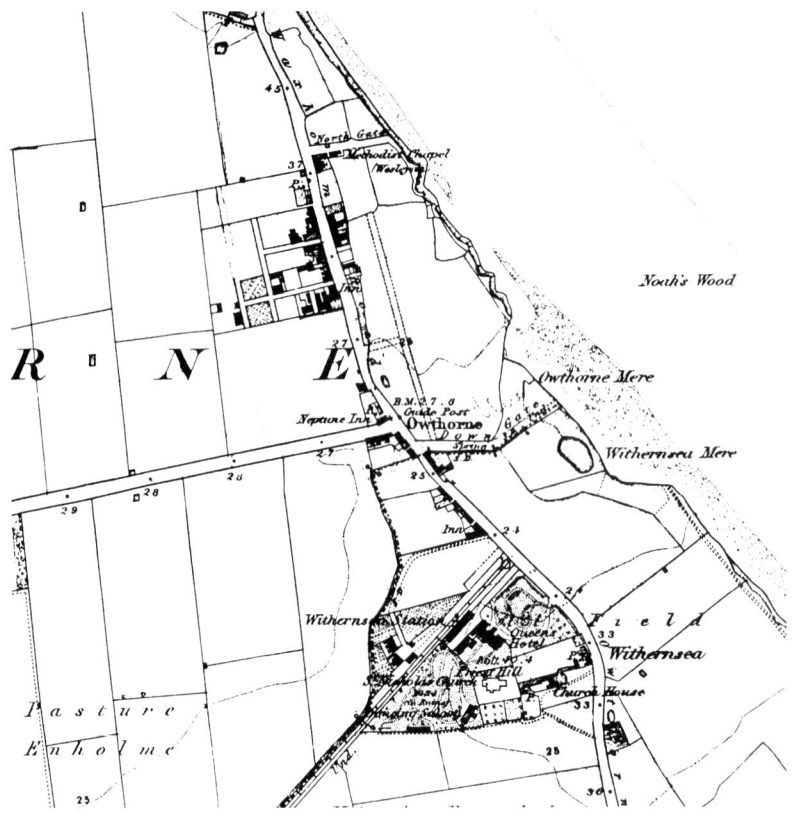

The coast of Holderness where the vanished village of Owthorne is still remembered by a small hamlet north of Withernsea.

Mrs. Mott. He then turned to rescuing the body of the mother for a christian burial but it was too late, she had already vanished in the waves.

An hour or so passed and there appeared to be no hope of further survivors. From debris it appeared the ship had been the *Adam Alvin* bound for Hedon from London. Returning to the vicarage he found the motherly Mrs. Mott had already washed and dried the baby boy and placed it in warm clothing by the fire. The following Sunday Enoch christened the child and named it Adam Alvin after the ship which had foundered. He decided to keep him in his household rather than hand him to an uncertain future in the hands of parish officials.

As the years went by the three children in the vicarage grew up together with little other company of their own age, Hull was the nearest town of any size and the roads were so bad that journeys there were seldom made.

Apart from having a smaller bedroom Adam was treated in all respects the same as the two girls and the vicar gave them their education together. Despite this the Reverend Sinclair rather naïvely assumed the young boy would realise his place in life and not have expectations beyond his station. This was not so and, when at the age of twelve the boy was called aside by the vicar and told it was time he went to work it came as a thunderbolt to the lad. He was told gently that he could either be sent as an apprentice to Hull, work on a local farm or become the vicar's manservant. Choking back his distress the boy chose to remain in the vicarage.

Succeeding years saw Adam acquit himself well in his new post. A strong and vigorous personality and an increasingly handsome young man, he soon impressed himself upon the two nieces and it became obvious Mary had fallen deeply in love with him and he with her. By 1707 they were openly courting much to the Rev. Sinclair's dismay. He considered that it would not only be an improper match, but that Alvin would be unlikely to be able to support his niece in a proper manner. When, as he had feared, Alvin approached and asked him for Mary's hand in marriage he refused point blank and ordered them to stop seeing each other. Rather stupidly as it turned out the vicar allowed the young man to retain his job and continue living in the vicarage.

Mary and Alvin were determined they should have their way and soon persuaded Catherine that their uncle was being miserably unreasonable. In the winter evenings of 1707 after the vicar had gone to bed the trio plotted in secret. At Adam's instigation they decided to do away with the elderly clergyman.

Spring came and went with Summer thunderstorms brewing. At 5 o'clock on what had been a dark stormy 10th June, while the two girls trembled downstairs, Adam went to his saviour's bedroom carrying an undertakers spade. As he entered the room his victim wakened and querulously asked what he wanted. Adam said nothing but at the sight of the menacing spade the unfortunate clergyman cowered in his bed and begged for mercy. Giving no sign, Alvin dragged the frail figure from the bed and struck it a mighty blow with the spade and continued to belabour the twitching form until all life had gone.

Callously dragging the body downstairs Alvin ordered the now terrified girls to go and clean the bedroom while he calmly dug a grave beneath the brick floor of the study and buried the vicar's body in a large grain sack.

As daylight began to break Alvin saddled the vicar's horse and took it on to the muddy land leading to the village of Paull. Allowing the animal to go free he then dropped the murdered man's wig and hat in a nearby ditch. Later the same afternoon he reported to William Dewlove the parish constable that the household feared some harm may have befallen the Reverend Sinclair. He explained how the vicar had set off on his horse the previous day and had not returned. A group of men were soon mustered to mount and search the area and before long the straying horse and the other evidence was found. It was immediately presumed the elderly man had fallen to his death and been washed out to sea. The local coroner agreed and a verdict of death by misadventure was returned.

The ordinary villagers of Owthorne were not convinced that foul play was not involved particularly as few liked or trusted the arrogant Alvin. He, worrying the body might be discovered dug it up and with the help of the girls, reburied it in a pit only a few yards from the vicarage.

On the 29th August 1707 Adam Alvin married Mary by special licence at Halsham church. The couple moved to live in London and Catherine, a shadow of her former self since the murder, went to live with an aunt in the quiet backwater of Patrington Haven.

The Alvins started a small business with money inherited by Mary, and Adam soon became a familiar figure in the city inns, ever ready with a wager and quick wit. But all the time he nursed the fear the secret might come out and was particularly concerned about Catherine who was now out of his reach. Had he but known it he did have real cause to fear his sister-in-law's state of mind as she became more and more withdrawn and depressed at the village on the Humber.

Unbeknown to Catherine, Adam and Mary moved back north and took up residence at Grimsby across the estuary from where she lived. Still worried about her Adam decided to visit Patrington Haven and one calm night he rowed across the treacherous waters of the Humber and appeared unexpectedly before Catherine and her aunt. He said Mary was very ill and he wanted Catherine to go back with him to look after her. Much to her aunt's surprise Catherine refused point blank and cowered away from Adam. Thinking it was the dangerous crossing she feared the aunt tried to put the girl's mind at rest but to no avail.

When Adam reluctantly departed the aunt admonished her niece for her uncaring attitude when to her surprise the girl burst into tears and sobbed, "I was afraid he meant to murder me like he did to Uncle Enoch!" The truth was out and a horrified aunt immediately took the girl to the authorities to tell her story. It was 10th April 1712, five years after the murder had occurred.

The girl took the constables to the spot where Alvin had buried the body and a grisly skeleton was soon revealed. It was properly buried in the chancel of Owthorne church a few days later. Alvin was arrested and taken to York Castle strenuously denying any responsibility. Throughout his trial he continued to protest his innocence at times with considerable skill and always with vigour. Unfortunately his histrionics lost him the court's sympathy while the two sisters were considered to have been acting under his overpowering influence. He was found guilty and sentenced to death.

On the eve of his execution Alvin was allowed to receive the last sacrament and, in keeping with tradition, a clergyman from his area in this case Mr. Mace, vicar of Halsham, was enlisted to preach an execution sermon. Mr. Mace chose for his theme a condemnation of the heinous crime of murder and in the middle of his pious homily Adam Alvin suddenly rose up and, to the amazement of those present made a vehement and passionate claim of his innocence. So affected was the Reverend Mace that he suffered a heart attack and died on the spot. Never one to let a chance go by Alvin immediately thundered that this was a sign from God and shouted "See, the hand of God visibly displayed!"

The rest of the congregation were visibly affected by this dramatic incident. The authorities were less impressed however, and the following morning the condemned man Alvin contritely confessed his guilt and sought forgiveness before being sent to meet his maker.

The few buildings left at the then village Owthorne clung precariously to the crumbling cliffs but by the middle of the nineteenth century all traces of it had been claimed by the sea which had so nearly taken the life of the baby who became Adam Alvin.

The records of the births, the deaths and the marriages of the little hamlet called Owthorne still survives but, like the building themselves, all traces of the name Adam Alvin have been obliterated!

DICK TURPIN - HIGHWAYMAN & MURDERER

Arguably the most famous highwayman in our history, Richard Turpin, while not a native of this area is bought within the province of this book because he concluded his life of crime in the Welton district of East Yorkshire. Far from being the somewhat romantic and chivalrous figure often portrayed Turpin was a cruel and cunning horse thief, housebreaker and murderer. Even the fabled ride to York on Black Bess is largely fiction and involved not Turpin but a contemporary Richard Nevison who, being suspected of robbery in London, fled to York on one mare, completing the journey in one day.

Son of a farmer in Thackstead, Essex, Richard Turpin was apprenticed in Whitechapel after being educated at a common school. While still quite young he married a Miss Palmer of East Ham but not before he had already started on a life of crime.

Beginning with petty thieving he soon turned to stealing cattle where previous butchery training stood him in good stead in disposal of the animals. Stealing mostly from neighbours he quickly slaughtered the beasts, cut them up and sold the meat, His luck ran out when he stole two oxen from a Mr. Giles of Plaistow two of whose servants immediately suspected Turpin. When they went to his home however they could only find a lot of unidentifiable meat. Convinced of his guilt they persevered and found the animals' hides at Waltham Abbey having been sold there by Turpin. Once sure they informed the parish constables who went to Turpin's house to arrest him. Seeing them approach, Mrs. Turpin informed her husband who, realising he might be in difficulty, escaped through the back window.

Unable to return home he arranged for his wife to bring him money and he joined a gang of smugglers. This association finished when Customs officers attacked the gang and its members split up.

Moving to the wild area of Epping Forest, Turpin soon joined a gang involved in stealing deer. With Turpin's encouragement they widened the scope of their activities and started breaking into houses. The method they chose was to knock on the door of the selected dwelling and when it was opened, usually by a servant, they all rushed in screaming and shouting oaths and brandishing weapons. This usually succeeded in terrifying all those in the house and it became a simple matter to steal whatever took their fancy.

Their first success was at the home of a Mr. Stripe an elderly shopkeeper in Watford who they robbed of a considerable sum of money. Spurred on by this success Turpin told the gang he knew of an elderly woman at Loughton reputed to have £800 in the house. On arrival the maid opened the door and cowered away in terror as the desperate bunch rushed inside. They proceeded to blindfold both the maid and her elderly mistress and asked the latter where the money was. Receiving no reply Turpin threatened to set her on fire if she didn't tell and, when the woman again resolutely refused he told the gang to sit her on the roaring fire. Despite being seated on red hot coals the woman still bravely kept silent until the heat began to reach her skin. With a cry of terror she indicated the hiding spot and the jubilant gang made off with £600.

Farmhouses were found to be particularly good targets. Not only were they isolated and free from interruption but farmers had a justifiable reputation for storing large sums of money in their homes.

Sometimes Turpin acted with mock gallantry and bravado as when they attacked the farm of Mr. Sheldon at Croydon. After binding and gagging the coachman, Mr. Sheldon was found in the farmyard and forced to hand over eleven guns together with jewellery and plate. Later Turpin returned two of the guns together with a note apologising for the inconvenience of the raid. By contrast the increasingly brutal behaviour by the gang was shown in the attack on the home of an elderly Mr. Lawrence at Stanmore. The night was dark when they rushed in the servants' entrance after their knock had been answered. Rounding up the terrified staff they bound and gagged them before seeking out the frail owner of the house. Blindfolding him they demanded weapons and on discovering none stole money and plate. Still not satisfied Turpin bundled the trembling old man up stairs and demanded more. Threats of murder having no effect one of the gang took a kettle from the fire and threw the scalding contents in their victim's face. A further search of the house revealed a girl servant cowering in the dairy where she had been working at the time of the raid. Despite her pleas she was taken upstairs and brutally raped.

Such was the anger aroused by this incident the King himself was informed and issued a proclamation calling for the criminals' apprehension and offering a reward of £50 and a free pardon to any of the gang willing to give evidence against his fellows.

Undeterred the gang committed a similar offence in February 1735 at Marylebone but so great was the furore that two of their members were immediately captured and summarily hanged and the rest were forced to split up. The reward was increased to £100.

Turpin took the road towards Cambridge and on the way met a gentlemanly figure on a splendid horse. As they drew alongside Turpin suddenly drew his pistol and demanded money. To his astonishment the other threw back his head and roared with laughter. "What? dog eat dog?", he eventually spluttered, "come, come brother Turpin, if you don't know me I know you and shall be glad of your company!" His name was King and he was already famous as an intrepid highwayman.

The two struck up a partnership and started working together. So great was their success and their fame so widespread that no inn would take them in. Finding a cave in Epping Forest screened by bushes and large enough to take them and their horses they established a base from which they operated as highwaymen. Mrs. Turpin supplied their food and clean clothing.

They worked amicably together although they had different attitudes. One day at Bungay in Essex they spotted two pretty young woman being paid £14 for some corn. Turpin suggested they get the money but King demurred from attacking two young girls. Not persuaded, Turpin insisted and they robbed the two.

Although known as a desperate man the £100 was nevertheless a tempting bait to many and in 1737 Thomas Morris, a forest worker set out with a friend intent on catching Turpin and claiming the money. Turpin saw them coming and noticing their guns thought they were poachers. "There are no hares around here" he called. "No," replied Morris raising his gun, "but I've caught a Turpin!" Calmly Turpin kept talking as he backed to where his own gun lay loaded and primed. Swiftly seizing it and before the others realised his intentions he shot Morris dead and the other man ran away. He had committed his first murder and a royal proclamation was issued offering a free pardon plus £200 reward for any accomplice willing to turn Queen's evidence against him.

Turpin left the area and went in search of King again and found him working with a highwayman called Potter. The trio made their way towards London and when nearing the Green Man Inn in Epping Forest they met a Mr. Major riding a most splendid horse. Turpin looked at the animal enviously as his own horse was very jaded and on the spur of the moment he drew his pistol and made the man change horses. Mr. Major was very well connected and his anger spurred the authorities into action. Guessing who the trio were and their likely haunts, the stolen horse was eventually found at the Red Lion in Whitechapel. Keeping the animal under observation the constables were rewarded when a man subsequently identified as King's brother called to collect it and he had a whip bearing the name Major! Promised his freedom if he helped in locating the wanted men King's brother pointed in the direction of Red Lion Street. Going straight there the constables immediately saw King who tried unsuccessfully to fire his gun at them. The weapon misfired and the constables seized him. Seeing Turpin approaching King called out to him to shoot the men holding him. Turpin fired and hit King. "Dick, you have killed me!" cried King as he staggered and fell. Panicked by the sight Turpin pulled his horse round and made off at a fast gallop.

It was a week before King died and during that time he was full of remorse for his way of life and eager to please his gaolers. He indicated Turpin would very likely be at Hackney Marsh but men sent there missed him. They were told he had ridden away the previous night loudly lamenting that he had killed his friend.

For a time he skulked about in the area of Epping Forest by now constantly hunted. On one occasion bloodhounds were used in an effort to catch him but Turpin recalling the exploits of King Charles in a similar predicament, climbed an oak tree and watched in terror as the slavering dogs passed underneath. The experience so frightened him he decided to get clear of the area and make for Yorkshire.

As he approached Long Sutton in Lincolnshire he took the opportunity of stealing some grazing horses but was caught in the act. The worthy parish constable, a cobbler by trade, was proudly taking his prisoner to the magistrate when Turpin knocked him to the ground and made off. He found his way to Welton on the banks of the Humber in the south western corner of the East Riding.

He established himself in the area as a gentleman and used his wife's maiden name of Palmer. He dealt in horses and cattle but unbeknown to the locals his stock was generally replenished by his frequent forays into neighbouring Lincolnshire to steal animals.

He was welcomed by the local gentry to join them when they went shooting game but it was returning from one such occasion which started the sequence of events which eventually led to his downfall. For no apparent reason Palmer shot and killed a fine cockerel belonging to his landlord. Mr. Hall, a neighbour who was with him at the time, remonstrated with him and Palmer turned on him and snarled, "If you stand still I'll shoot you too" Offended and frightened by this behaviour Hall reported the matter to the Welton parish constable who immediately sought out a Magistrate and obtained a warrant for Palmer's arrest. When the warrant was executed Palmer was taken to Beverley to appear before the Quarter Sessions there.

For what appeared to be a minor matter the justices were happy to bind Palmer over to be of good behaviour but, unfortunately for him he was unable to find a surety for his future conduct. Confining him in the Beverley House of Correction the magistrates began to hear stories of his visits to Lincolnshire and rumours that he might be a horse thief and even a highwayman. Palmer, in answer to questions said he had been an unmarried butcher living in Long Sutton with his mother and sister but had been forced to flee from debts.

Writing to Lincolnshire the clerk of the peace discovered a man Palmer had escaped custody there for horse stealing and this so concerned him he had arranged for George Smith and Joshua Milner to take the prisoner immediately to the security of York Castle where he was placed in 28 1lb chains for the next four months while investigations were made.

A couple from Lincolnshire travelled to Welton and identified a mare and foal belonging to Palmer as having been stolen from their premises. Meanwhile Palmer wrote to his brother in Essex entreating him to get some good references for him from London. He failed to pay sufficient postage on the letter however and when it was delivered his brother declined to pay the excess. It was languishing in the local post office when it happened to be seen by Mr. Smith who had been Turpin's schoolmaster. He immediately recognised the distinctive handwriting and informed the authorities. The letter was opened and from its contents it was deduced that Palmer in custody at York and Turpin were one and the same man.

Rid:g of Yorks.   THE Information of James Smith of Th——
                   in Essex taken upon Oath before George Nel[thorpe]
                   John Adams and Thomas Place Esquires this 22.th
                   day of February 1738.

This Informant sayth upon Oath before us. That he this
Informant saw a Letter directed to one Pompr. Rivernall
of Hempstead in Essex with the York Post Stamp upon it
and the said Rivernall refusing to take the Letter in
this Informant acquainted One Thomas Stubbing of
Bumpstead Helion in the County of Essex Esquire who
sent to Saffron Walden Post Office and payd the postage
And this Informant upon perusing the said Letter had a
Suspicion that it was Turpins hand writing, And four
of his Majesty's Justices of the peace in the County of
Essex desired this Informant to go to York Castle to see
whether it was the said Turpin or not who Says upon Oath
before us That the person now Shown to this Informant
is Richard Turpin and no other person. And this
Informant is the better able to know the said Turpin
by being bred and Born in the same Town with him
and also went to School with this Informant and has
Constantly for several years since been in Company
with him till within this three or four Years, And further
Saith That the said Pompr. Rivernall Marryed one
Dorothy Turpin the said Richard Turpin's own Sister.

                                            James Smith

Taken upon Oath before us
three of his Majesty's Justices
of the peace for the West-
Riding of Yorks: the day
and Year above mentioned.

           T. Place
           Geo. Nelthorpe
           Jn. Adams

The Information of James Smith identifying Turpin at York.

Local magistrates arranged for Mr. Smith to travel to York where he was taken round the Castle and immediately identified Turpin from among all the prisoners.

The news broke that the infamous Dick Turpin was in custody and crowds flocked from all over the country to see the celebrated criminal and a great national debate took place whether in fact Palmer and Turpin were one and the same. One young man who claimed to know Turpin well visited the prison and after a long period of studying the man offered a wager of half a guinea to the gaoler that it was not Turpin. "Take his wager", whispered Turpin to his gaolor, "and I'll go halves with you!"

Finally tried before a Judge at Assize Turpin faced two charges, was found guilty and sentenced to death and, once the die had been cast and although not giving up hope of a reprieve Turpin began to face his fate with great equanimity and considerable courage. Attempts by his father to get persons of quality to speak for him failed, but refusing to show signs of distress the condemned man gaily arranged for ten poor men to walk as mourners behind the sledge carrying him to the scaffold. He bought new shoes to wear at his execution and distributed a number of hat bands and gloves to folk in the area. He also left a ring and some other valuables to a married woman of his acquaintance in Lincolnshire.

It was Saturday 17th April 1739 when the moment came and Richard Turpin alias John Palmer alias John Pawner stepped on to

Richard Turpin's gravestone in York.

the execution cart with a jaunty step and, as it made its way to the gallows followed by the pathetic band of mourners he waved and bowed gaily to the crowds. It was recorded that "he had an air of the most astonishing indifference and intrepidity".

Prior to ascending the scaffold it was noted his right leg was trembling and he stamped it irritably as if ashamed it may be taken as a show of fear. After talking to the executioner for thirty minutes Dick Turpin threw himself into eternity and the folklore of his country.

The body was taken to the Blue Boar in Castlegate and next day it was placed in a coffin and buried in St. George's churchyard. Despite being buried extremely deep to avoid body snatchers within twenty-four hours the grave had been desecrated and the body stolen. When news of the outrage spread the population of York were so enraged they took the law into their own hands and soon located the body at the house of a local surgeon It was recovered and reburied, this time the coffin being filled with quick lime.

BLACK DEEDS AT BENINGBROUGH HALL

Beningbrough Hall, on the banks of the river Ouse to the north of York had a turbulent early history. Originally the land belonged to religious orders but was seized by Henry VIII and eventually ended up in possession of the Bouchier family.

Descendants acquired the reputation of being increasingly mad, they fell out with the crown and were fined and occasionally imprisoned for offences. During the civil war they fought for the Commonwealth and a Bouchier was one of those who sentenced Charles I to death. At the time of the restoration there is little doubt Bouchier would have been hanged and his lands forfeited but he cheated the gallows by dying. His son professed to be a strong royalist and was allowed to retain the estates.

In 1768, there being no male heir, Beningbrough passed to Margaret Bouchier who married the amiable but romantic Giles Earle. He had spent many years in France, particularly Paris where he had become involved with emissaries of the French government who were supporting those American colonists who were seeking independence from the English crown.

After his marriage to Margaret and inheriting of Beningbrough Earle continued to conspire with the Frenchmen and is believed to have secretly sent a quantity of arms to support the rebel colonists.

Learning that the authorities had become aware of his activities he immediately suspected his one time friend and co-conspirator — Col. Brackard. He confronted him and a duel was arranged at which the Colonel was fatally wounded.

At the time we are speaking of the Earle household consisted of some twenty servants headed by Marian Dukes the housekeeper, Philip Laurie the steward and Martin Gale, head gamekeeper.

Marian was a most attractive and capable 22-year old woman who had risen in the Earle's service since she was 12-years old. Over the years the family had come to trust her implicitly and depend upon her considerable ability in running the household. For the previous two years she had been courted by Martin Gale, a bachelor who had been recruited to the estate some four years previously from the large Londesborough Estate near Pocklington. He lived on his own in the gamekeeper's cottage some hundred yards from the Hall.

Philip Laurie, between 30 and 40 years old, darkly handsome, and an ambitious young man who had slyly ingratiated himself into the family with his willingness to please. Since becoming steward the Earles had begun to suspect his loyalty to them was not what they expected. He too had designs on Marian and was secretly jealous of her relationship with Martin Gale. He also sensed and resented the special trust in which the family held Marian and it rankled in his mind. Outwardly he was calm and smoothly friendly, inwardly he seethed and planned ways of revenging imagined slights. Although a bachelor the steward had sought and received permission to live in lodgings in the nearby village of Newton.

With the possibility of his arrest becoming greater Mr. Earle decided to take his family and leave the house, travelling first to London and then on to the continent where he felt he would be safe until he could return. Unable to take much luggage with him and fearing his house and valuable contents could be seized by the authorities, he discussed the matter with Marian. At her suggestion they decided upon a plan which would require the co-operation of Martin Gale.

The Earles left and some ten days later two heavily muffled gentlemen arrived from London and, to the surprise of Laurie the steward, claimed to have instructions from Mr. Earle. Laurie was told to gather all the servants together and when this had been done the younger of the two men addressed them. All the silver, paintings and other valuables were to be removed from the house! Laurie was on the point of refusing to allow this when Marian spoke for the first time. She said should could vouch for the two men and knew they had Mr. Earle's authority. Furious at this further example of Marian's privileged position Laurie nevertheless knew he had to obey.

The local ferryman had been summoned with his boat and the property was loaded aboard and taken away. Suspiciously Laurie watched the constant ferry trips and decided the goods were not being taken very far. He therefore walked cautiously along the river bank following the ferry on one of its trips and found, to his astonishment that it was only going some 400 yards, the boat was then unloaded and all the property moved to the gamekeeper's cottage, the home of Martin Gale.

The work done, Mr. Earle, for it was he who was the second of the men, departed with his friend for London. A few days later he travelled to France and settled down there to wait.

Back at Beningbrough as the weeks passed Laurie's desire for Marian and his jealousy of Martin grew into an obsession that the two should not marry. He began to visit low class areas of nearby York and struck up an acquaintance with a William Vasey well known as a ruthless criminal. After a while he got Vasey to agree to murder Marian and arranged lodgings for him in Newton.

Vasey discovered the young woman usually took a short walk on the river bank each afternoon and so he made his plans. It was a lovely day and Marian took no notice of the lone fisherman as she strolled along the bank. It was not until she was about to pass him that the figure sprang up and violently attacked her. Despite her terrified struggles his strength was such he was able to stifle her screams and force her into the river where he held her head under the water until her struggling stopped. The body was found floating downstream on the outskirts of York a few days later and in the absence of any evidence to the contrary a verdict of accidental death was recorded. She was buried in the churchyard at Newton-on-Ouse.

A distraught Martin Gale gave evidence at the inquest and said it was unthinkable that Marian had accidentally fallen into the river but was unable to provide any other reason for her death. The villagers and estate workers fed by rumour discreetly fuelled by Laurie, began to think Gale might have murdered Marian during the course of a lover's quarrel.

Still not satisfied with his work and eager to become wealthy, Laurie decided to take advantage of his master's absence and he told Vasey about the valuables at the gamekeeper's cottage. Together they planned to steal as much as they could carry and Vasey said he could dispose of it. Because of the number of folk around during the daytime the attack would have to be at night when Gale would be asleep.

At midnight on a moonless night the two conspirators went to the cottage and Vasey quietly forced a front window open. As arranged he entered the house while Laurie kept watch outside. Bludgeon in hand he crept to the rear of the house where he knew Martin Gale was sleeping. As he opened the bedroom door Gale, still restless with worry about Marian, heard the latch click and jumped out of bed. Immediately he received a tremendous blow on the head which knocked him to the ground and he almost lost his senses. He found himself fighting for his life and another savage blow struck him but still he didn't lose consciousness. Summoning his not inconsiderable strength he raised himself and grasped Vasey in an iron grip around the throat. Despite his attacker's frantic struggling Gales's muscles had been hardened by a vigorous outdoor life as a gamekeeper and, slowly but surely he pushed Vasey into the front room where, still grasping the throat he managed to open a window, seize a nearby gun and discharge it. The noise of the report terrified the watching Laurie who made off as servants from the house, roused by the noise, arrived at the scene and Vasey was detained.

Samuel Clark the parish constable and Robert Wycombe a local magistrate were summoned and arrangements were made to transfer Vasey to York. He was committed for trial on a charge of burglary with intent to murder, convicted and sentenced to death. Before the execution was carried out, in a vain effort to obtain salvation he admitted a long list of crimes including the murder of Marian.

Some months later, while Mr. Earle continued to live abroad, with no action being taken against him, Mrs. Earle decided to return to Beningbrough with the children. She had heard of the desperate happenings on the estate and on her return began to suspect that Laurie was somehow involved.

She summoned the steward and questioned him at great length and with considerable skill. The man squirmed and writhed under her penetrating questions and used all his ingratiating skills to convince her of his loyalty and innocence of the dreadful happenings. He tried hard to hint that the real instigator had been Martin Gale. Not satisfied and thoroughly disgusted by his whining performance Mrs. Earle told him he was dismissed forthwith. Thunderstruck, Laurie stood speechless before her and then, with blood suffusing his face, his temper seemed to snap and he snarled as he pulled a pistol from his pocket and fired it at point blank range at his mistress.

Fortunately, because of their close proximity and her rapid reactions, Mrs. Earle was able to knock the weapon off line just before it fired and the bullet passed by her head. Laurie turned and rushed away as the shocked lady of the house fought to recover from the shock. The parish constable and some bailiffs were summoned and a hue and cry was immediately mounted for Laurie's arrest.

Men went immediately to his lodgings in Newton and found the door locked. Quickly breaking it down they found the body of Laurie, lying across the bed, a still bleeding wound in the head and the pistol clutched in his hand.

Upset by the awful events at Beningbrough Margaret Earle returned to France to her husband. Although they did return to Beningbrough for short periods, they spent most of the rest of their lives travelling in Europe. On her death early in the nineteenth century the house and estate passed into the possession of the Reverend W. H. Dawnay.

MURDER AT LECONFIELD

It had been a busy Christmas for colour manufacturer Mr. Pennock Tygar in 1822. He had a factory at Grovehill near Beverley and he was out working right up to the evening of Christmas Eve. His wife had been due to spend Christmas with her mother at their farm at Driffield Wold but had cancelled the arrangement because of her husband's business. However on Boxing Day Mr. Tygar told her she was to go and stay with her mother the next day for a week or so. Her half hearted protests falling on deaf ears, the early hours of Friday 27th December saw her happily preparing for the journey. Mr. Tygar had arranged for his servant Richard Walker to drive his wife in the gig to Driffield and return the same day. Starting early in the morning they made good time and Richard started his return journey on foot at 11 o'clock. He never reached Beverley. Richard Walker was a nervous young man who two years previously had been employed by Mrs. Harrison, the mother of Mrs. Tygar, at their farm at Driffield Wold as a groom.

One evening while staying there Richard was sitting up for Mrs. Harrison who was absent when he heard a noise in the yard. Going outside he said he saw a man he knew to be William Johnson of Kelk who ran away on seeing him. Richard aroused the household and it was discovered the granary had been broken into and some bacon stolen.

A warrant was issued for Johnson's arrest but he remained free for some time and when apprehended and placed before the Magistrates was able to convince them with an alibi for the night in question.

A day or two after the court hearing Richard Walker was exercising some horses in a lane near the farm when he saw Johnson who was apparently waiting for him. Johnson came up to him and swore violently and said he blamed Richard for his court appearance and that he would get his revenge even if it took him twenty years to do it. The meeting terrified the nervous groom and he began to be depressed and nervous and unwilling to go anywhere unaccompanied, particularly after dark. Meanwhile Johnson was gaining a reputation in the neighbourhood as a violent and brutal man whom few would tackle.

Mrs. Harrison realised her groom's increasing nervousness and depression was rendering him virtually useless as an employee but she was reluctant to lose him because he was such a good worker. Mr. Tygar of Beverley, having recently become her son-in-law was looking for a new groom and so it was decided he should take Richard Walker into his employ.

Since then the young man had worked well and his confidence had returned somewhat although Mr. Tygar knew better than to send him out at night without another worker with him. Consequently when the trip to Driffield Wold arose Mr. Tygar was careful to ensure the groom started at 7.0 am. He would easily arrive at about 9.0 am and after refreshments be able to leave to walk back as he had to leave the gig at Driffield. He would arrive at Beverley easily in daylight before 4.0 pm and Mr. Tygar arranged for a worker from the factory to meet him outside North Bar and walk with him to Grovehill. These were kind and very considerate arrangements which would have worked had it not been for Walker's own foolishness.

Arriving at Driffield Wold with Mrs. Tygar he was given some food and he drank a fair quantity of strong Christmas ale which might have given him more courage. He started to walk home and on entering Driffield who should he see but Johnson who came across in an unexpectedly jovial mood. Holding out his hand he said, "Now Dick, let's be friends and forget all I ever said to thee. I'm sorry we aren't friends — let's have a glass of ale together." Whether taken in by Johnson's changed manner or because of the Christmas ale will never be known but Richard Walker went with him and stayed drinking in the public house until two o'clock.

When he finally set out for home Johnson accompanied him saying he had business with a farmer at Beswick. But the cold air seemed to sober Richard up quickly and all his old fears returned. Seeing an old man who he knew breaking stones on the roadside he went back to him on pretext of getting a light for his pipe. This involved striking flint and steel and took some time and Richard told the man of his fears. The man advised him to turn back to Driffield for the night but at that moment Johnson called to him to hurry up and fearing he would be branded a coward he carried on towards Beverley.

Gommery Hall between Scorborough and Leconfield

The two reached the Vernon Arms at Cranswick and here they had some more ale before heading once more for Beverley. Reaching Beswick they entered the Hare and Hounds, famous for its landlady Grace Darling whose mulled ale and smiling face were known to every bagman who rode the Scarborough Mail between that town and Hull. Seemingly overcome by a terrified fascination for Johnson, Walker took more ale here and it was not before an hour and a half had passed that the by now staggering groom left once more for Beverley.

At about 7.0 pm a servant girl was chopping wood at the back of a farmhouse known as 'Gommery Hall' at the corner of the footpath leading to Lockington in one direction and Leconfield and Scorborough in the other when she heard a distinct cry of 'murder'. She listened and the cry was repeated twice more. Alarmed she ran into the house where the other servants were at supper and told them. They came outside and listened but heard nothing. Telling her she had mistaken an owl's cry they resumed their supper. To their amusement the girl refused to change her story.

Johnson's eventual and terrible confession describes what happened:- "Directly I saw him at Driffield I made up my mind that I would murder him, and seeing he had been having some drink I thought my task would be easier. I determined to act in a friendly manner towards him as it would save me a lot of bother. I got him into the Blue Bell and had a glass of gin; and then again we called at Cranswick and got some more. By this time he had got almost more than plenty. I did not drink much myself. I was full of devil and very impatient at what appeared to me as most unnecessary delay. By the time we got to Beswick he had almost walked the drink off, and talked about the robbery at Mrs. Harrisons and I laughed and said I had forgotten all about it and that we had better let it drop. We were now opposite the Hare and Hounds and I said, "We will go in and have some of Grace's mulled ale, it will help us to walk better". He agreed and we went in. I called for a quart and I let him have the greatest share. He appeared to be fond of the drink after he had tasted it and when we started off he staggered in his walk. I said, "As it is a fine night we will go by the foot trop (footpath) to Scorbro'. It will be a shorter walk." He seemed to have forgotten I had said I wanted to see a farmer at Beswick which place we were now leaving behind. My object was to get him off the highway. He fell at once into my views complaining about being tired. As we went along through the fields the temptation came on me and I picked up a stone and was waiting for an opportunity to strike him on the temples with it to stun him and just as I was raising my hand with that intention I heard something stir. It was a man and a woman sat through the fields the temptation came on me and I picked up a stone and was waiting for an opportunity to strike him on the temples with it to stun him and just as I was raising my hand with that intention I heard something stir. It was a man and a woman sat on stile we had to pass. Had they not have stirred his life would have been saved. As it was it only put off the event for a short while and I quietly dropped the stone and after telling them it was a fine night we crossed the stile and walked

View from Gommery Hall towards Scorborough Church.

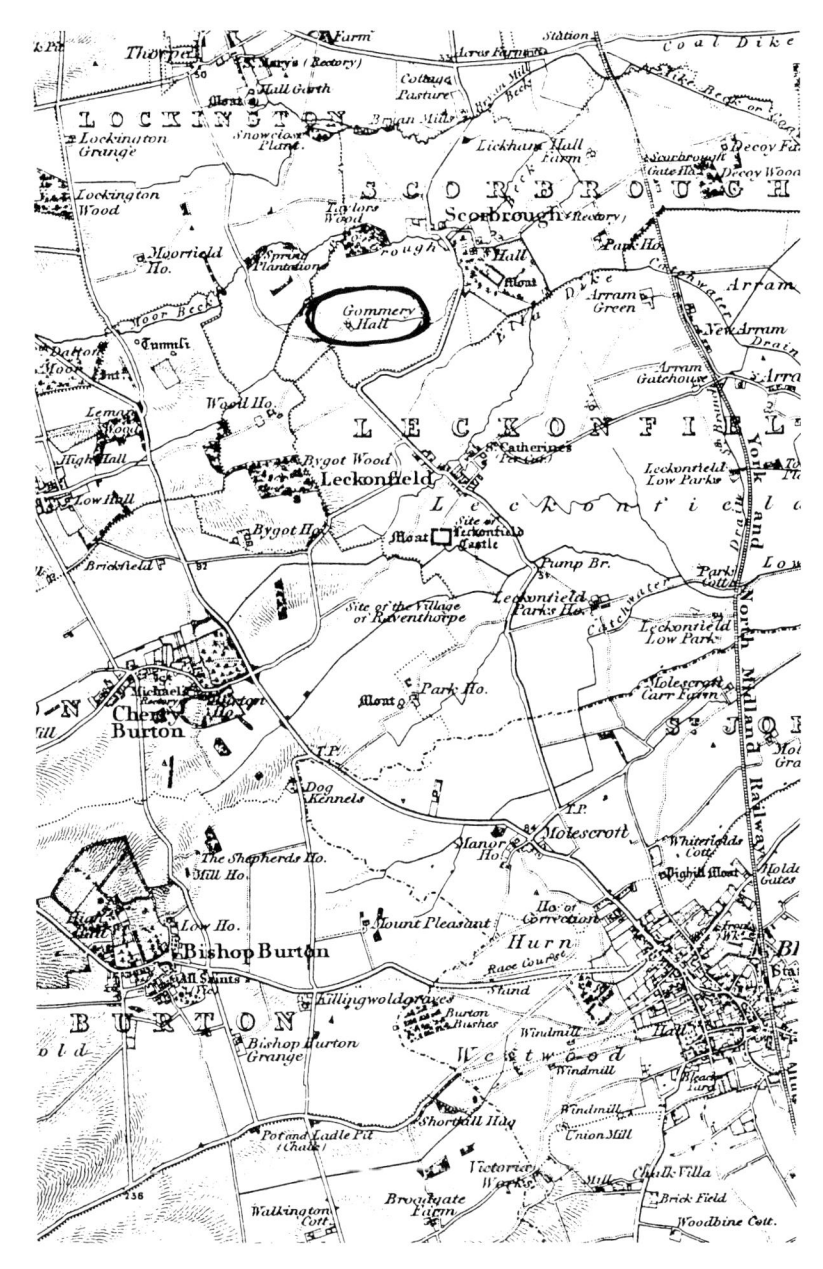

Map of Scorborough/Leconfield area showing Gommery Hall.

on towards Scorbro'. I did not stop at the pub at Scorbro' but we again took the foot trod over the fields in the direction of Leconfield. By this time a mist had come on and it was so dark we had lost the foot trod and I stumbled against some netting where some sheep were eating turnips. I put my hands out to save myself and felt a net stake. The idea at once entered my head, why not use this? It will make a short job of it. Unseen by Dick I wrenched it from the ground and walked with it behind me till I came to the next stile which, being a low one, I jumped over. (I forgot to say he always asked me to get over stiles first lest I should attack him from behind.) As he was getting over in his drunken way I struck him on the forehead with the stake, but as he was staggering at the time, he bowed his head and the blow did not tell (*sic*) as I wished it to do. It seemed to sober him and he closed with me in a desperate clutch which caused me to drop the stake which he tried to prevent me from reaching. I am a very strong man. I scarcely ever met my match but fear lent him strength and he nearly mastered me in spite of all I could do to prevent him. We struggled and fought over the field until we reached the next stile. Had he crossed it he would have been only four fields from Leconfield and within reach of help, which his cries might have brought. We were now opposite 'Gommery' Hall and he had cried 'Murder' once. This raised all the devil within me and I struck him with all my might. He cried 'Murder' twice more. I could hear the barking of the yard dog at the farm house and seeing he was reeling I struck him again with all my remaining strength and he fell to the ground with a groan. I then kicked him in the face and he appeared to faint. I then ran back to where I had dropped my stake and it lay ready for my hand. I returned and with it beat his forehead as he lay on his back with his face upturned to the sky. One blow I struck cut off his right ear from his head. Being fearful he might still live after I had left him despite his fearful wounds I took out my pocket knife and cut his throat. As I was wiping it on the grass the church clock was striking seven. I stripped him of his coat, waistcoat and shirt which I tied up in a bundle along with his hat in a large handkerchief which I had with me and I tossed him into a ditch and then went on my way back again. I have read of men being haunted by the ghosts of those they have killed. I was not — it never troubled me at all. I was glad I had served him out. I have never cared about being found out."

Unaware of all this Mr Tygar in Beverley was becoming more and more agitated at the non-arrival of his servant as he had no way of knowing if his wife had arrived at her mother's home. Eventually, unable to contain himself the businessman went to the town lock-up and informed the chief constable.

It was too late to see anything that day so arrangements were made for the road to Driffield to be searched at daybreak. The news of the disappearance soon spread throughout the town and a traveller reported he had seen Walker earlier that day on the Driffield to Beverley road, about five miles from Driffield and he appeared to be on his own. Mr. Tygar was beside himself. Where was his wife? Could Walker have dropped her off and been on his way back to Beverley?

At last morning came and the search party started out on roads and footpaths. As they left the village of Leconfield, James Smales one of the borough watchmen recruited for the search gave a shout. He had found something in a ditch! It was Walker's body, almost naked and with a cut throat!

While looking round the scene the Leconfield parish constable John Arram was smart enough to spy a single button in the mud and he gave it to the chief constable.

Enquiries made from other travellers revealed that Walker had been seen about three or four miles from where his body had been found at about 5.0 pm on the 27th. He had been with another man who the travellers recognised as William Johnson.

Enquiries to trace Johnson were difficult as he normally tramped the country in the manner of some ex-soldiers who were still vagrants some seven years after Napoleon had been defeated at Waterloo. He was known locally as not only a violent person but to be an odd young man, short and stout with a very round, flat face and a permanently sullen look which made him appear stupid. Physically he was phenomenally strong and he had a voracious appetite. Eventually he was arrested when he visited his mother's house and he appeared to be wearing some of the clothes missing from Walker's body. It was also discovered he had sold a watch similar to one owned by the dead man, to a jeweller in Driffield.

He denied all knowledge of the crime and claimed he had been in Driffield all day on the 27th. When tackled about the clothes he was wearing he said he had bought them in a London market some three weeks earlier. Unfortunately for him one button was missing from the coat and those remaining matched exactly with the one found at the murder scene.

Despite his denials when he appeared before the Magistrates at Beverley Courtroom, Johnson was committed to York Assizes charged with murder and he pleaded not guilty. After a lengthy hearing the jury convicted him on circumstantial evidence and he was sentenced to death. Smiling, the condemned man left the dock, shook hands with prisoners waiting below and promised to bequeath his braces to one of them.

He remained calm and apparently content with his lot as the hours ticked by to his execution. A scaffold was erected behind the Castle and on the evening before he was due to die the chaplain visited him and to his great surprise Walker said he wished to confess to the murder and to ask forgiveness. It was then that he told his gruesome story. Afterwards he slept soundly all night and at eight o'clock on Monday 24th March 1823 he smiled at the executioners as he mounted the scaffold and went calmly to his death.

A macabre footnote to the savage murder was that Johnson's body was given up for dissection and Dr. Sandwith of Beverley obtained his skull which was placed in his surgery with the word 'Johnson' cut into the forehead.

JEALOUSY AT THE FARM

The evening of Monday 14th April 1856 was mild and there was a definite and welcome hint of Spring in the air as Thomas Bell and his wife made their way home to the farm at Grindale. It was his birthday and they were returning from a successful visit to the market at Burlington, or Bridlington as it was to become known in later years. The light was just failing as they reached the house.

Although they had no family their home seemed full of people as they entered. In addition to servant girl Fanny Wilkinson, busily preparing the evening meal, there was Thomas's foreman, John Hebblethwaite and shepherd George Stephenson, both of whom lived in at the farm.

Thomas wearily slumped into his chair in the parlour with the two other men while his wife went to attend to things in the kitchen. Fanny the maid came up to him and said, "Anthony White the carrier brought you a hamper today from the station —I'll go and get it." She returned with a box and opened it and to Thomas's surprise it contained a stone jar with the name 'T. Kay, Wine and Spirit Merchant' on it. Thomas had dealt with them for years but hadn't ordered anything. The jar was corked and roughly sealed with wax.

Addressed to Thomas in writing he didn't recognise, he wondered who might have sent it. He told Fanny to uncork it and looking in saw the jar was only partly filled with a liquid which looked and smelled vaguely like wine. He wondered if it might have come from his father-in-law in Lincoln who had, on one previous occasion sent him an unannounced bottle of champagne.

Pouring some into a tumbler Thomas smelt it again and wrinkled his nose in slight disgust. Then he gently tasted the liquid and swirled it round in his mouth. It tasted better than it smelt but somewhat unsure of himself Thomas spat it out.

"Taste this" he said as he passed the glass to Fanny and then to the two workmen. Fanny spat her's out but both men drank small quantities. Thomas then took a glass to his wife and she took a tiny sip but said she didn't like it.

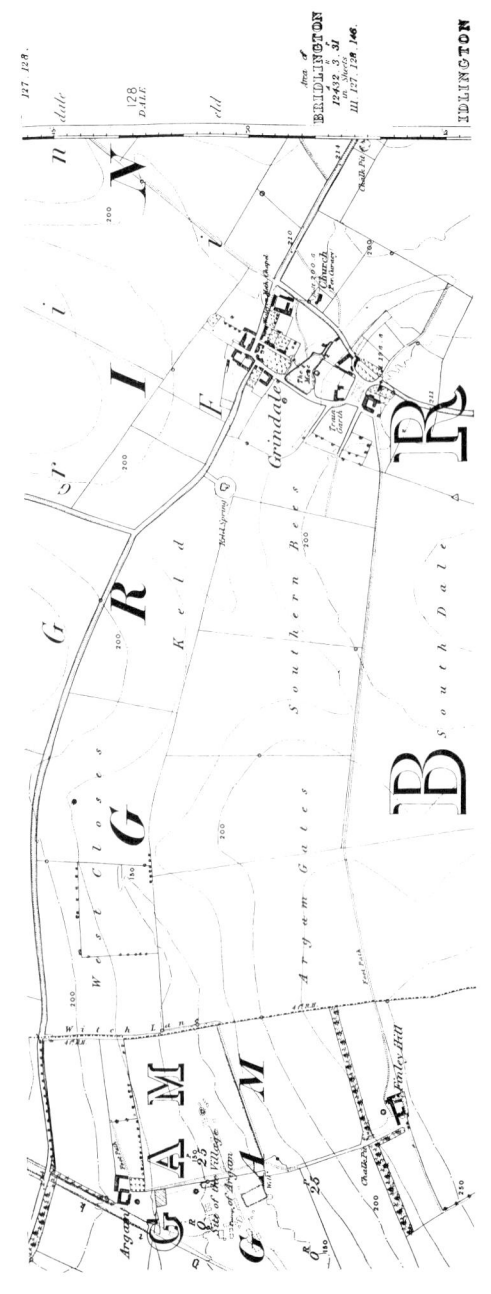

Showing Grindale, Finley Hill and Argham

One of the men shouted to him to return to the living room and when he got there they were trying to comfort Fanny who was sat in a chair looking extremely distressed. She was deathly pale and shivering uncontrollably. When he felt her brow she was stone cold. Thomas instructed his wife to give the girl brandy and after a while the trembling ceased. Fanny broke a lot of wind and began to sweat profusely. Mrs. Bell put the girl to bed and when she appeared to be sleeping peacefully the rest of the household retired.

Next morning everyone had splitting headaches and the bottle and its contents began to seem more sinister. Taking the bottle with him Thomas left the farm and made his way quickly in his gig to Burlington where he called at the home of Mr. Hutchinson, a surgeon. Explaining the situation he asked the medical man his opinion on the liquor.

The surgeon was later to tell a court how he took the container and, extracting some liquid from it, injected three ounces into the stomach of an unfortunate cat. The animal died after 15 minutes of violent convulsions. Still uncertain the surgeon injected 1 drachm into a two-month old rabbit which expired in 15 seconds. An older rabbit took 45 seconds to die and the surgeon was "surprised the last animal did not shriek like the others!" He told Thomas a strong poison was involved and suggested further examination be made by a chemist in York.

On his way back to Grindale Farmer Bell called on the local police sergeant Thomas Southwick at Hunmanby and told him the facts. The startled sergeant who had never before received such a serious

The approach to the hamlet of Grindale.

complaint enquired if Bell had any idea who might have wanted to harm him or his family. "Only one", said Thomas, "my brother George from Finley Hill!" "Why do you say that?" asked the sergeant and Thomas spent the next half hour describing a situation common in many families where property is involved.

He related how he was the youngest of four children, two boys and two girls but was by far the hardest worker of the family. George, his elder brother had always been something of a wastrel with a tendency to drinking and particularly to gambling. When their father died in 1853 he overlooked George and left the family farm at Argham to Thomas who was a bachelor at the time but with a caveat that should he die childless the property passed to George or his heirs.

The rest of the family were enraged but, were even more incensed when, a year after their father's death, Thomas married a Miss Sharp from Lincoln. His sisters refused to attend the wedding and lost no chance of being unpleasant to their new sister-in-law.

Although George had remained on speaking terms with his younger brother, Thomas was sure it was only so that he could use him. He constantly pestered for loans and only in February that year had asked to borrow £200 but Thomas had lent him only £100. Thomas did not trust his brother and felt that if anyone would do him a mischief it would be him.

Sergeant Southwick saw Thomas Bell out of the police cottage and immediately got on his cycle to ride to Burlington where he informed his Superintendent of the allegations. Told to investigate the matter he started by ensuring Mr. Hutchinson sent the bottle's contents for further checks and then went to see Anthony White the 14-year old boy who was the carrier between Grindale and Burlington.

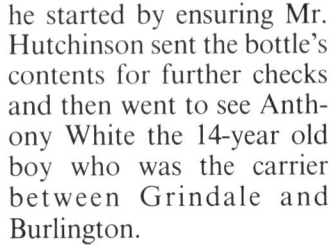

White remembered collecting the box from David Burrell the ostler at The Globe Inn in Burlington which was where all packages for Grindale were collected, and delivering it

The farm at Argham.

to Fanny the maid at Mr. Bell's house. When he saw Burrell the sergeant learned the box had been delivered from the railway and that it had originated at Hunmanby station. Francis Speck the station master also remembered the package and recalled sending it on to Burlington as it was addressed to Mr. Bell at Grindale. He could not say who had delivered it to Hunmanby station as it had been found in the shed.

Asked if he had ever carried anything for George Bell, Anthony White the carrier had related how some weeks previously he had received a strange request from him to obtain a bottle of gin from Kay's the wine merchant. He was not to purchase it himself but to get the Globe ostler to buy it and to tell no-one who it was for. Burrell confirmed the story and also the fact that the bottle was similar in shape to that which was delivered to Thomas Bell's home.

Sergeant Southwick had arranged for police in Burlington to check other chemists in the town and, lo and behold, one, William Smith recalled George Bell visiting his shop and asking for highly toxic prussic acid to be put into some phials he was carrying. The chemist had laughed at him because he only supplied prussic acid on a doctor's orders. However, because he was busy he had to allow his apprentices to serve Bell and he couldn't be sure what they gave him.

By now the police had only one link missing before they had enough circumstantial evidence to charge George Bell. Who had delivered the parcel to Hunmanby railway station? If it had been George then the case was pretty well complete even if he didn't admit it. It was Thomas Bell's opinion that his brother would be unlikely ever to admit to any wrong.

As expected the whole area was buzzing with gossip and rumour about the case and nowhere more so than in the public houses in Burlington. One of the regulars at the Globe Inn was Jacob Tranmer who was a shepherd for George Bell having previously worked

47

for his brother Thomas. A shifty and unreliable man he was nevertheless a hard worker and Thomas had been disappointed when he declined to be re-engaged when the last Michaelmas hirings had come round. Since the rumours about the attempted poisoning Tranmer was noticed asking a lot of questions about stories of a reward for any information — some said fifty pounds was on offer. He hinted to the landlord that he might be in line to receive the money.

Police, ever vigilant in the pubs, soon heard of this and Sergeant Southwick found Tranmer in the pub one evening and tackled him about the case. Initially very cagey and after enquiring about reward money, Tranmer eventually said that his master George Bell had asked him one evening to take a package to Hunmanby railway station and leave it there. He was not to hand it directly to anyone. Some days afterwards Bell had enquired if in fact he had delivered it as instructed and when he said he had done so his master had expressed doubt and said "if I had they would have been off by now". He didn't know who 'they' were and he hadn't noticed the address on the package.

Although police knew that Nathan Sharp, Thomas Bell's father-in-law had actually visited George Bell and accused him of attempting to poison his brother's family and that George had denied it, it was nevertheless decided Tranmer's evidence clinched the matter and Sergeant Southwick was told by his Superintendent to apply for a warrant to arrest George Bell and then they could question him when he was in custody. Very early on the morning of 1st May Southwick, alone but armed with an arrest warrant, visited Finley Hill. His knock was answered by George who was bleary eyed and still in his night shirt. "George Bell, I have a warrant for your arrest!" announced the sergeant, "You will come with me". The bleariness vanished from Bell's face and he said he would go upstairs to change. "You can't go upstairs," said the sergeant, "you must come". Bell persisted and the sergeant relented and said he could go and put some clothes on but that he would go with him. On reaching the bedroom Bell complained that modesty prevented him from changing in the sergeant's presence but the officer refused to budge. Just then Mrs. Bell called to the sergeant from downstairs and he went to the top of the stairs to see what she wanted. On his return a few seconds later the window was open and his prisoner had vanished! The crestfallen sergeant who had done so well to

The house at Finley Hill.

investigate the case thus far had lost his man and was not to see him again for a long time. He had no idea which way Bell had gone and could only make his weary way back to Hunmanby.

Unbeknown to him Bell had made his way across the fields and spending the first two days hiding in barns and woods eventually went to the house of his brother-in-law, Thomas Hodgson. He told Hodgson he was fleeing from some creditors who he feared would be violent towards him and asked his help. On 4th May Hodgson took him in his gig to Hessle station and they boarded a train to Liverpool. On reaching the port and having said his farewells George booked a passage on a vessel about to sail for America. On his return home Hodgson told his wife she had seen the last of her brother.

In the autumn of the same year however rumours began to filter into the district that George had returned to England, some said he had never left and that he had been seen in Sewerby outside Burlington. Eventually it was learned that a man answering his description was keeping a shop at Wakefield in the West Riding.

Fearing a repeat of the previous attempt to arrest him it was decided by Major Granville-Layard, newly appointed chief constable of a very new East Riding constabulary, to send the most impressive of his Superintendent to bring George Bell to book.

Yorkshire Spring Assizes.

[MARCH 21, 1857.

THE ATTEMPT AT POISONING, NEAR DRIFFIELD.

Superintendent Joseph Young, stationed at Great Driffield was not a man to be trifled with and, although his service was to be noted for many indiscretions he was unlikely to be out-witted by any escaped prisoner.

The Superintendent duly arrested Bell at Wakefield on 25th February 1857 and he appeared at York Assizes on 18th March. Never having admitted the offence despite the strong circumstantial case against him, George pleaded not guilty and the case unusually took a whole day. He elected not to give evidence himself and so subject himself to cross examination, but relied on his counsel to put doubts in the juries minds about the prosecution's case. Tranmer was a drunk who could not be relied upon said his counsel Mr. Seymour. Why on earth would George Bell want to kill his brother? How could it be proved that the parcel George had despatched to Hunmanby was the one which had been delivered to Thomas? As for his client's running from the police — this was simply because he had understood it to be connected with his indebtedness. He concluded his address with an eloquent appeal, urging the jury to give the case their most earnest, serious and charitable consideration.

After the Judge had addressed them the jury retired and returned after an hour to announce they found the prisoner guilty but they recommended mercy for the sake of his wife and family. Mr. Justice Crompton said morally speaking the crime Bell had committed was not less than that of murder and if death had resulted he would have been on his way to execution — "a sentence which would, without the slightest doubt, have been fulfilled". While always paying attention to juries' recommendations for mercy, in the present case he could see no reason why mercy should be extended to the prisoner, whose case, in his opinion, was by far the most serious and dreadful to be tried before these Assizes. He therefore thought he was only fulfilling a public duty which devolved upon him in sentencing George Bell to be transported for the term of his natural life!

CHEATING THE HANGMAN IN BEVERLEY

Queen Victoria was in the middle of her reign over dominions far and wide and in England the little town of Beverley was snuggling prosperously beneath the towers of its awe inspiring Minster. Situated just north of the Humber estuary and already somewhat overwhelmed by its burgeoning neighbour Kingstston-upon-Hull, its citizens were nevertheless proud of their ancient borough and many were merchants of substance.

One such was John Maister who lived in considerable comfort and decorum at Register House in the middle of town. He kept a number of servants to attend to the needs of himself and his family and among them was 34-year old Henry Baker, a gardener. Quiet and inoffensive as far as his master was concerned, the widower with three young children was thought to be a somewhat withdrawn and brooding figure by the rest of the staff. A sound worker he seemed to become more morose when his wife died.

Thirty-year old Ellen Hatfield had moved from her home in Pocklington in her teens to take up a position as maid in the Maister's household. Barely five feet tall she was extremely pretty and people wondered at her having remained unmarried for so long. In truth she seldom looked at a man although plenty gave her more than a sidelong glance. All this changed when Baker began paying attention to her and it was soon obvious to the other servants that Ellen had fallen for the reserved widower and that he was becoming more and more possessive towards her,

In fact the gardener became so jealous of his new girl friend he resented her going anywhere without him and when she went to spend a few days with relatives in Nottingham he escorted her to the station and took the train with her to Hull where she had to change. He wrote letters every day she was away and remonstrated with her if she failed to reply.

Notwithstanding Baker's unhealthy possessiveness the two became engaged and the marriage date was fixed when suddenly, to Baker's dismay, Ellen said she wished to postpone the wedding.

On the afternoon of Friday 23rd October 1857 Ellen Hatfield left

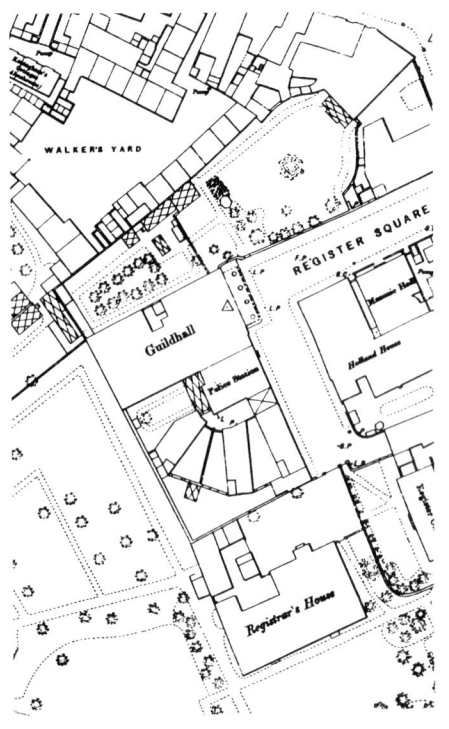

Register Square Beverley, With Register's House and garden.

the house in Register Square as it was her free afternoon and it was assumed she had gone to see her fiancé. Unusually she failed to return at tea-time and Mrs. Hardy, the cook, became very concerned. She sent a messenger to Baker's house who returned some half an hour later having found no sign of the gardener or Ellen.

Now, thoroughly alarmed, the cook alerted the rest of the household and as daylight was failing it was decided to inform Mr. Robinson the town gaoler. He made a cursory search of the heavily overgrown garden at Register House and found nothing. A decision was made — police would have to be involved and Superintendent Dove, Sergeant Dunne and Constable Robinson arrived at the house which no-one could remember being in such a complete turmoil before. The Beverley Borough police were quietly excited by the thought that a really serious crime had occurred in their area and set to work with a will to search the garden at Register House properly.

Although prepared for the worst, Constable Robinson, on hacking his way under an overgrown apple tree, recoiled in horror. Lying in front of him was the fully clothed body of a young woman with the whole of her body and the surrounding undergrowth covered in blood. When he pulled the branches away from under the body the head appeared to fall from its neck and revealed that it was completely severed apart from the spinal cord.

Looking up, the officer realised that had it not been for the undergrowth the dreadful scene would have been in full view of the

Magistrates' Room in the Town Hall.

Calling the other officers they made a further search together and, a few yards away found the body of Baker, he too having a slashed throat. However unlike poor Ellen he was still alive although scarcely breathing.

The local surgeon Mr. Boulton was called and he pronounced Ellen Hatfield dead. Her body was removed to the mortuary. He ordered Baker to be taken into Mr. Maister's house to the dismay of its owner, and it was found he had recovered consciousness but was unable to speak. He asked for a slate and with difficulty wrote a confession. He said he had asked Ellen to marry him forthwith, she had refused so he had cut her throat and dragged her to where she had been found. He had then attempted suicide. Realising Mr. Boulton was having considerable success with his ministrations he refused to be treated by him and Mr. Wardle, another medical man, had to be called in. Each time he visited Baker, Mr. Wardle expected to find him dead but he lingered and lingered.

A week later Baker was still living and to the delight of his gaolers apparently getting stronger until he started refusing food and was obviously determined to die. The authorities meanwhile seemed similarly determined to keep him alive for the machinery of justice to take its course and commenced to forcibly feed him.

An Inquest was held on Ellen Hatfield at the Golden Ball Inn and after hearing all the evidence the jury announced Baker guilty of wilful murder and he was committed to the next York Assizes.

The trial was three weeks away and the battle continued between Baker and his gaolers for his life. Every day appeared to be his last but then he would rally. A tube was daily forced into his throat and liquified food forced down it. Baker fought with what strength he had remaining to prevent the food being forced into him and gradually the authorities realised they were battling uselessly. Although they got food into the man, no sooner had they withdrawn the tube then he vomitted it back again.

Two days before the Assizes were due to sit Baker died. Before he did so he again asked for a slate and wrote,

"I took the life of the one that I loved, I should like to see my dear mother, sister and brother. I hope I ham (sic) the same son to my mother though a graceless one. I cannot talk to anyone that they can understant (sic) me what a pity it is that I should have spoiled my voice so."

Once again a tragically unnecessary ending of two lives.

CRUEL MURDER IN HULL'S FISHING FLEET

Life aboard any fishing vessel was probably as hard as one could get anywhere in the nineteenth century. It was made even harder by the violence always waiting to burst from men facing the elements. One of the most notorious cases which came to light resulted in the death of the ship's boy, William Papper at the hands of his skipper, Osmond Otto Brand.

Brand was a 27-year old Hull man, skipper and proprietor of the *Rising Sun* fishing smack operating from the port. Among the crew was the 14-year old lad — William Papper. Also from Hull, he was described as a cheerful boy and an obedient shipmate.

The boat left Hull for the North Sea fishing grounds on a bitterly cold 16th December 1881 with Brand, two seamen and three boys. The youngest was Papper and he was deputed to be cook. As they sailed it appears Papper passed by Brand and, innocently remarked that his sister knew the skipper. For some reason this apparently innocuous remark caused Brand to react with a campaign of unbelievable ferocity against the youngster. During the course of the voyage the skipper, and all the crew except for one young apprentice, subjected Papper to the most savage treatment.

When the vessel returned to Hull on 15th January, Brand reported to police that while the vessel had been about 120 miles off Spurn Point, the cook, a 14-year old boy William Papper, had been knocked overboard by a sail and, although the boat had been put out and a search made the body was not recovered.

However soon afterwards two members of the crew reported the true story to the police and as a result Brand was arrested. Their story which stretches the imagination to believe was revealed in court.

The brutality towards young William had begun soon after leaving port after the mention had been made of his sister and the captain. Brand ordered Papper down into the cabin and crewman William John Dench of Staniforth Place, Hessle Road, stood on the ladder. He heard Brand say, "Now you bastard, I'll pay you for telling lies about me! I've had something to do with your sister have I?" He then began to thrash the boy with a knotted rope swearing and cursing as he did so. Brand finished by slashing the boy across the face with the rope causing blood to spurt. The lad was very badly hurt.

When about 90 miles from Spurn some damage was caused to the fishing nets and to the crew's surprise Brand turned to Papper and said "That's all through you" and struck him in the face, knocking the lad to the deck. "Get for'ard and stay there for three days!" the skipper ordered and the crying lad began to move towards the bow. Then Brand shouted, "Get up on the stem", but Papper was unable to climb up because of his condition. "I'll make him," shouted Brand and got a bucket which he filled with sea water and emptied over the sobbing boy. He did this five or six times until Papper cried out, "Please don't throw any more water over me and I'll get up." He climbed onto the stem. Brand then gave him a hand spike and told him to hold it and to say, "If I had not been a bad boy I should not have had to do this."

Later Brand was seen to throw the boy off the Stem and onto the deck. Told to get up Papper tried to do so but fell down again. Brand bent over him and struck him with his fist and when William struggled on to his knees he struck him with a rope which he then tied round him. He called to a crewman named Blackburn and said "Come and heave the bastard up".

With the rope over the cross trees of the boat Papper was hauled up until his legs were four feet from the ground. Brand pulled on his legs and the trees broke. Dench said to Brand, "You've done a nice thing now you nearly hung the lad!" "Well, the cross trees is the worst" replied Brand.

A few days later Brand, for no apparent reason, knocked a terrified Papper to the deck. He then jumped on the hapless lad, tied a rope round his neck and pulled it tight. Dench went up to him and told Brand to leave off. The skipper replied, "I don't care, I'll kill the bastard". Dench untied the rope as Brand pulled out a knife and said to Papper, "I'll cut your liver out!"

On New Year's Day, the lad who had been kept on deck for days, complained of feeling dirty and infested with vermin. Ordering him to take his clothes off, when Papper was undressed Brand told Dench to throw a bucket of sea water over him and he did the same. Brand then told the shivering youth to go below and he would give him some dry clothes. Papper was so cold he couldn't get the socks on so Brand struck him with a knotted rope.

Unbelievably the savage and unrelenting treatment continued. On

William Papper, Otto Brand and three other crew members of the 'Rising Sun'.

one occasion Papper was reported to be below sitting on a bucket. "I'll haul him up", said Brand and at his order crew went and tied a rope round the boy and before he was hauled up some filthy substance from in the bucket was wiped across his mouth.

When the pathetic figure was hauled to the deck he was tied to the side and the crew poured buckets of sea water over him. Later as the exhausted boy was trying to work on the nets Brand said, "Say your prayers you because you won't live another day on this Smack!"

The desperate boy crept below when the skipper was not looking but was soon found and dragged out. "Put him in the Dill" shouted Brand and the poor boy was lowered with difficulty into a sort of well in the bottom of the ship. Young William managed to sit down in waist high water when Brand decided to jump in on top of him. Dench said the boy should be brought out and as he was being raised up Brand hit him repeatedly with a lump of wood. At that moment the fog horn sounded and Brand said, "There you bastard the bell's tolling for your death!" He then knocked him down and jumped on him. Leaving the boy lying on the deck Brand went aft.

Dench went to Papper and found him lying against the windlass with his eyes blackened and his face horribly disfigured. He told Brand he thought Papper was dying. "A bloody good job too" was the only response. Then he said, "We can't take him into Hull, his face is all disfigured." The boy was carried into the cabin and Brand said, "We'll put him in some canvas and throw him overboard — it's alright, he's only shamming!"

Sometime later Brand told Dench the boy was dead. Dench went below and saw the lifeless body on the bunk covered with some sort of netting. Brand said, "It's alright you're all in this as well as me!" Dench retorted, "You put most nails in his coffin". "I don't think I have, you've all done your share," retorted the skipper. The crew put the body of Papper over the side and when they docked Dench heard Brand tell Papper's father that he had been knocked overboard by a sail.

Although Brand was the instigator of the savagely pursued persecution of a defenceless lad some, if not all of the crew joined in from time to time and could not be considered totally blameless.

Without their evidence however a case could never have come to Court and Brand was found guilty of murder and on the 22nd May 1882 was hanged at Leeds Prison for one of the most brutal cases of murder ever to have been committed on Hull's fishing fleet.

THE DEEMING CASE

One of the most notorious characters with whom Hull's detectives were involved was Frederick Bailey Deeming. Not a native of the town, his first appearance in the area was when an apparently wealthy man named Lawson, appeared in the Hull and Beverley areas. Said to be recently returned from Australia he let it be known he was a sheep and cattle rancher in that country. Not particularly good looking he nevertheless dressed very well, spent a lot of money with Hull and Beverley traders and, stayed in the best hotels.

Before long he struck up an acquaintanceship with a young single lady — Nellie Matheson who lived with her widowed mother and sister in their house at New Walk, Beverley. In no time Mr. Lawson became a lodger in the Matheson house and, in the new year of 1890 was married to Nellie by the Reverend Canon Quirke at St. Mary's church.

Prior to the marriage some local people had already become suspicious of Mr. Lawson and their suspicions increased when they learned he made secret journeys to Market Weighton to collect his mail! Unfortunately these apprehensions did not reach the Matheson household and, the newly wedded Nellie arrived at Hull's Royal Station Hotel for her honeymoon. On their arrival Mr. Lawson left her in the bedroom and never returned.

In fact the man had become aware that police making enquiries concerning certain of his dealings in Hull were closing in on him. He had purchased considerable amounts of jewellery from Reynoldsons of Whitefriargate and, the cheque he had issued had been found to be worthless. He travelled directly to Southampton and, it was later discovered, left the country on SS *Coleridge* bound for South America.

The distraught Nellie, on realising she had been deserted, returned home to Beverley where another, even greater, shock awaited her. A woman arrived who said she was a Mrs. Frederick Deeming from Birkenhead and that it was her husband who had purported to be Lawson and gone through a form of marriage with poor Nellie. They had a family and had recently moved to Birkenhead. She knew what had happened because her husband had told her! He had telegraphed and asked her to deny being married to him if police arrived and asked questions. Outraged, she had immeiately travelled to Beverley.

Detective Sergeant Grassby who was dealing with the case in Hull, made urgent enquiries and sent messages for the *Coleridge* to be intercepted at the first possible port. This transpired to be Montevideo in South America. Lawson was arrested there and, because no extradition treaty existed with Uruquay for bigamy the Hull fraud charges were used.

Frederick Deeming.

Sergeant Grassby travelled to Montevideo and spent a long trip escorting his prisoner home. During this time he found Lawson alias Deeming to be an exceptionally difficult and vicious man to deal with.

Lawson received a sentence of nine months imprisonment for the Hull offfence and was released from Hedon Road prison in July 1891.

Sometime later a major enquiry began in Liverpool when a woman and four children were found murdered at Dinham Villa, Rainhill. The house had been recently rented for the family by a man giving the name Albert Oliver Williams. It transpired Williams had been seen at the house one day when the mother had taken the baby out. Startled neighbours heard shrieks of terror which were apparently made when he was murdering the three elder children. On the mother's return Williams felled her with a stick and slashed the tiny baby's throat while still in its mother's arms.

A great hue and cry was raised and it was discovered Williams had sailed from Hull to Antwerp in SS *Zebra*. It was thought he may have gone on to Australia but enquiries were difficult to pursue satisfactorily at such a distance.

Then a number of coincidences took place. A Hull skipper went to have his photograph taken in Antwerp and saw a photograph of a man who had previously been a passenger on his ship the *Zebra* to Belgium and who had called himself Lord Dunne. He had claimed to be a very wealthy self-made man from Australia but, most passengers were very suspicious of him. The skipper, intrigued by the circumstances, bought a copy of the photograph.

Deeming, alias Lawson, ever vain, had also had a photograph taken by Mr. Barry of Park Street, Hull to whom he introduced himself as an M.P. So suspicious was Mr. Barry he insisted on a deposit before taking the photo!

Eventually the photographs and the man using the names Williams and Lawson were tied up as one and the same person but, little progress was made in locating him until the most amazing coincidence of all occurred.

Harry Webster, the Governor of Hull Prison, retired. His doctors recommended it would be beneficial to his health if he moved to Australia to live. When in Melbourne he was reading about a murder in that city and was struck by the description of the man in custody. He also thought the circumstances of the murder were very similar to the Rainhill case which had been heavily publicised prior to his leaving England. After some debate with himself he went to see the chief constable of Melbourne and subsequently identified the man in custody as Lawson who had been in his prison in Hull for nine months.

Deeming, alias Lawson, alias Williams, alias Lord Dunne, was eventually hanged at Melbourne for the murder of his Australian wife. Before the execution he admitted the Rainhill murders. It subsequently transpired that, at the time, yet another girl was on her way to Australia to marry him and he had already dug her grave under the kitchen hearthstone in Melbourne! Nellie Matheson of Beverley had been a very lucky young lady!!

A CHAMPION MURDERER

The 1st December 1898 saw Mr. Justice Darling take his seat at York Assizes to hear possibly one of the most gruesome cases of murder to come out of the City of Kingston-upon-Hull, a place not unused to gratuitous violence. George Stoner, a commission agent from 72 Peel Street, Hull was brought before him and charged with murdering thirty-seven years old Emily Hall on Friday 22nd July that year.

Stoner, married with two children but separated from his wife, was well known in Hull and the East Riding as a champion racing cyclist who was regularly seen competing at the Botanic track where he was known as a quiet, likeable fellow.

Emily Hall, an orphan, had for five years lived as the common law wife to a man in the city until they parted and she became like many discarded women, more and more dissolute in her way of life. Her reputation was best indicated when the Judge rebuked witnesses at Stoner's trial who referred to her as a 'lady' and suggested she be called a 'woman'.

The events leading up to the trial started at about midday on a warm, sunny Friday in July. Frederick Inkson was barman in the almost deserted Flower Pot Inn run by his father when a man and woman entered and bought drinks. There was nothing unusual about the pair or their behaviour except that Inkson thought the man was a better class than his companion.

Later Frederick Gifford who knew George Stoner, saw him in the Theatre Tavern in Dock Street and he was accompanied by a woman who Gifford did not recognise but who appeared to be getting the worse for drink.

The same afternoon Robert Saunders, was waiting outside T. M. Roberts of Dock Street, where he was foreman, for the 4 o'clock Rully. He saw Stoner who he knew, with a woman, coming towards him. As they passed he could see the woman was pretty drunk and he called to Stoner, "You'll be alright there Stoney" and laughed. Stoner had looked back and just smiled, as if in agreement with the sentiment. The couple were next seen entering number 1 Princess

Row off Dock Street a lodging house of very doubtful reputation and run by a mean German woman — Elizabeth Shukofski who takes up the story.

"The couple came in and the man asked if they could have a room as his wife was unwell and needed a rest. About an hour and a half later the man returned downstairs and said he was going for a short walk as his wife was still sleeping. He did not return and two hours later I went to investigate and found the woman apparently asleep so I did not disturb her. However time passed and still the man didn't return so I went back upstairs to see if the woman had wakened yet. On entering the room I heard the woman groaning and I asked her what was wrong. "Undo my corsets" she said in a strained sort of voice, "he's done enough at me!"

"As I started to undo the corsets I was horrified to see blood start to pour from beneath them and then, for the first time I noticed a great pool of blood on the floor. I must have fainted because I don't know how much later I found myself lying in the woman's blood and she had gone very quiet. I screamed, got to my feet and dashed down to my niece who was in the kitchen. I told her to run to the druggist in Lowgate and get something for the woman. A few minutes afterwards she returned and said he could not help. We put the woman in a cab and paid him to take her to the Infirmary".

Emily Hall died at midnight and police were called by the Infirmary. Superintendent Emmerson, no stranger to sudden death decided at once that he had a murder on his hands and he arranged for an immediate and thorough search to be made of the room where Emily had been found. There was blood everywhere, on the floor, the walls and the washbasin had bloody handprints on it. According to Mrs. Shukofski a cake of soap was the only thing missing from the room and had gone from the washbasin.

Doctors reported the dead woman had suffered the most horrific

George Stoner.

Peel Street off Spring Bank, the home of Stoner.

injuries which had caused heavy bleeding. She appeared to have been subjected to a savage sexual attack which ended in her body being ripped open in the area of the sexual organs. The ferocity of the assault appeared to be confirmed when the post mortem examination shocked the hardened police surgeon as he had never been shocked before. Well inside the body and lying next to the kidneys was a tablet of scented toilet soap. Puzzled by its position he could only assume it had been forced inside the body through one of the ripped orifices.

Police investigators were so perturbed by the apparent mentality of the killer that they tried to keep the case quiet to avoid alarming the population as well as to prevent the person responsible being warned of their investigations. It was an impossible task, so many people already knew and rumours began to circulate wildly in the city. Fortunately they resulted in the man Saunders coming forward and volunteering the information about Stoner. Shown a blouse from the body he identified it as similar to the one worn by the woman he had seen with Stoner.

Sergeant Hotham took Saunders on a tour of Stoner's known haunts and it was not long before they came across him and the

STRANGE DEATH OF A HULL WOMAN.

MYSTERIOUS PROCEEDINGS.

SENSATIONAL ARREST.

CHARGE OF MURDER.

foreman from Dock Street pointed him out to the sergeant. He was arrested and his lodgings searched. A dark blood stained shirt was found under the bed. Elizabeth Shukofski picked him out as the man involved when she attended an identification parade at the cental police station. When he was charged with the murder however Stoner replied firmly, "I wasn't there, I have a complete answer."

The trial created the greatest interest and when it opened many barristers unconnected with the case were present in court. Twelve men were empanelled as the Jury who would hold the prisoner's fate in their hands. Considered particularly unsuitable for the female sex, no ladies were allowed in the court. When Stoner appeared he was pale with a growth of prison beard on his face. His plea of not guilty was made in a tremulous voice.

From the beginning Stoner admitted going to the lodging house for an immoral purpose but denied causing the injuries delibertately. He claimed that if he had somehow caused them accidentally then he did not intend to cause the woman's death. Although not directly stated by the defence it was inferred that Mrs. Shukofski might not have been as innocent as she claimed. Had not a man been taken to the Infirmary from her house only recently suffering from mysterious wounds? Why had she sent all the way to a Lowgate druggist when a number of physicians lived nearer? Why did she try to clean all the blood and other mess up before the police were called? Suppose for some perverted reason the deceased had required the soap to be placed inside her and it had become lodged and Mrs. Shukofski had been called to help?

It should be said that none of these suggestions were put directly to Mrs. Shukofski when she gave evidence — she herself claimed she thought the woman had suffered a miscarriage.

Defending counsel closed his case with a claim that the whole of the evidence was circumstantial and turning t the Jury he asked, "Can you be satisfied that the man before youin the dock had satisfied his lust with animal ferocity and then proceeded to hear his victim to pieces?"

At 5.15 with rain spattering the dome shaped roof and dim gas lamps flickering, the jury filed out to consider their verdict. Stoner sat motionless in the dock as if transfixed until a warder touched his shoulder and he was led below.

A mere 35 minutes later the jury indicated they wished to return and the court re-assembled. Asked if they were agreed upon their verdict the foreman said, "Yes my lord". "Do you find the prisoner guilty or not guilty?" intoned the court clerk. "Guilty of committing grievous bodily harm but without premeditation", replied the foreman. The twelve sat looking hopefully at the Judge fearful that he would reject their attempt to save the life of the man before them.

Not surprisingly Mr. Justice Darling immediately rejected the verdict as one unknown to English law. He told the jury that if the prisoner had committed grievous bodily harm that it must be assumed he intended the natural consequences of his act and the verdict should be guilty of murder. He instructed them to retire again and return with one of three verdicts — not guilty, guilty of manslaughter or murder.

Again the twelve retired and time passed, 30 minutes, 40 minutes, 50 and then the Judge returned because the jury indicated they wished to ask some questions. Again he gave them firm directions and tension mounted as the court waited for what was likely to be the final time. Mercifully it took only ten minutes before they were back.

"Guilty of murder" — the accused flinched visibly as he heard the words but he held his composure. The Judge quickly asked him if he had anything to say before sentence was passed and Stoner whispered, "No, I have not, only that I am not guilty." Quietly Mr. Justice Darling said, "You have been found guilty of the most revolting crime and there is only one sentence I can pass. You will be taken back to the place from whence you came and there be hanged by the neck until you are dead." A muffled sob was heard from the dock as Stoner was quickly led below.

Despite his predicament the condemned man remained remarkably composed, even cheerful, in the prison. He still maintained his innocence and almost imperceptibly at first, pressure began to mount for a reprieve. On 5th December it was announced the execution had been fixed for Tuesday 20th December and that the executioner was to be Mr. Billingham assisted by his son who he was training to be a hangman.

If any reprieve was to be granted it was normal for it to be announced the week-end prior to the hanging but Friday 16th December came and passed and those campaigning for him began to lose heart.

Meanwhile in the bureaucratic corridors of the Home Office in Whitehall, London, the wheels of the Criminal Department were turning on the Stoner case.

A petition from the condemned man had been received in which he reiterated his trial defence and complained he was poorly represented at the trial. The matter was sent from Home Office to Mr. Justice Darling for his urgent observations — time was fast running out.

The Judge replied that all along he felt the verdict should have been manslaughter and not murder as the Jury had found. Mr. Justice Darling felt the sentence should be remitted to one of Penal Servitude for life.

On receipt of these observations Home Office moved quickly and on 16th December a reprieve was signed and rushed to the prison. Stoner was informed two days before he had been due to die.

A postscript to this story is that Stoner served his sentence in exemplary fashion but, when after 13 years the Church Army suggested he should be released, Home Office refused to consider such a move until he had served at least 15 years.

In 1913 he was released on licence and in 1915 his licence restrictions were removed. His family in Hull had made it known they did not wish him to return to the city so he had made his home with relatives in Leeds. The last report about him was dated 1915 when he was still residing in Leeds, in the middle of friends and relatives, was married and his wife was expecting a child!

HEARTLESS CRIME IN HULL

Tuesday 25th March 1902 saw a large group collected outside the grim gates of Hedon Road prison, Hull. Mainly men but with a good proportion of women and even children jostling as they stamped feet and rubbed hands in the frosty chill. A subdued murmur of suppressed but excited chatter rose from the crowd as the prison clock crept towards eight o'clock. Then an eerie but expectant hush crept over the gathering. A second or two after the first chime from the clock a black flag snapped loudly open above the grey walls and a cheer rose from the watching crowd, only to be quickly suppressed as if they were ashamed of such a demonstration. Hull had executed a murderer for the first time since John Rogerson had gone to the public gallows in 1778.

Sarah Hebden had lived alone in her riverside home at 97 Hodgson Street in the teeming working class area of terraced cottages in the middle of the great port where crime and violence lived side by side with a wonderful community spirit. A busy little widow she was a methodical body who earned a reasonable living acting as an agent for the Royal Liver Friendly Society. Neighbours whispered that she always had between £5 and £10 in the house.

Thursdays were her collecting days when she visited her insurance clients and usually collected about five pounds, three of which she paid into the Society's office keeping the rest as commission. Also on Thursdays it was her practice after paying in, to visit friends either at Elloughton or Leeds. Her widowed sister Mrs. Bower who lived next door also collected for the Royal Liver.

On Thursday 28th November 1901 Sarah was due to visit Elloughton after paying in her collection and very early that morning a young girl called Jackson called on her to pay the family insurance dues. Receiving no answer to her knock she called at Mrs. Bower's house. Knowing how methodical her sister was she was immediately alarmed in case she was ill. After a while she contacted the Friendly Society and finding her sister had not called there she alerted the police.

Constable Ridsdale arrived and watched by a large and expectant

The forbidding façade of H.M. Prison, Hull, little changed in appearance since it was built.

crowd, forced the door open. The stench warned but did not fully prepare him for the ghastly sight. At the bottom of the narrow flight of stairs was the crumpled body of Mrs. Hebden and it was obvious she had met with a violent death.

There were three large pools of blood on the floor and the body was severely bruised and battered with obvious dents in the skull. One finger had been virtually pulled from the hand and another was badly dislocated. By the side of the body was a bent pair of fire tongs, a piece of which was later found beneath the corpse. Detectives called to the scene were happy they need look no further for a weapon. The police surgeon, Dr. Slater opined that death had taken place some hours previously.

Enquiries revealed that contrary to her usual practice of keeping valuables downstairs her insurance books were hidden upstairs together with two purses, one containintg £3.12s.2d. and the other empty. Again unusually, her tea caddy, normally on the parlour shelf was found under her bed and had been broken open apparently using the same fire tongs she had been killed with. Inside were a further two empty purses and a newspaper cutting relating to the conviction and sentence to six months imprisonment of an

Arthur Richardson for robbing his aunt in Brigg earlier in the year.

Detective Superintendent Chapman, head of Hull CID who had taken charge of the enquiry sent Detectives Cherry and Proctor to enquire about the cutting and they discovered to their surprise that the victim in Brigg was the dead woman's sister and that Richardson was the illegitimate son of the third sister — Mrs. Bower!

Lincoln prison confirmed that Richardson had been released on 20th November in possession of 9s.2d. cash and an old metal watch. It was also learned that Richardson had joined the regular army after being an apprentice in Hull but had been discharged for dishonesty while in India. He was reported as being a coldly calculating and ruthless criminal hidden behind a very cool, calm and personable exterior. He became number one suspect for the murder.

Arthur Richardson

News of the savage crime spread quickly through the city and police soon learned that Richardson had been lodging at the house of a Mr. & Mrs. Skelton in Faith Terrace, Walker Street since Friday 22nd November. Detectives Proctor and Cherry visited the house, found Richardson there and arrested him on suspicion of murder. He had over £10 cash in his possession together with a gold watch and a brooch.

Questioned about these Richardson claimed he had owned the £10 when he went into Lincoln prison and had palmed it to prevent seizure. He said he had pawned the watch prior to his sentence and redeemed it on release. He denied having seen his aunt since returning to Hull claiming he had been too frightened to meet any relatives because of the theft from his aunt in Brigg.

Enquiries with Mr. and Mrs. Skelton revealed a more suspicious story. Richardson had obtained lodgings with them saying he had a job at Reckitts. This turned out to be false. The day after the murder he had turned up in new clothes and asked if he could borrow a key to wind his gold watch. He mentioned a newspaper report that his aunt had been murdered and Mrs. Skelton asked him point blank if he had done it only to receive no reply.

Rulleyman William Fenton came forward and spoke of meeting Richardson on Hedon Road on the morning of the murder. He had plenty of money and claimed to have won it gambling. Mrs. Lakin the landlady at the Trafalgar Inn in Blackfriargate recalled the prisoner talking about the murder and said he thought it would remain undetected like lots of other murders in the city.

Despite intense questioning by police Richardson stuck to his story and denied having seen his aunt let alone murdering her. When confronted with evidence of bloodstains on his clothes he maintained they could have come from a nose bleed or even from a fight he had been involved in before he went to prison.

Every jeweller in Hull was visited with the gold watch and eventually the investigators struck lucky when William Morely a watchmaker identified it as one he had repaired a number of times for the deceased woman. Confronted with this damning evidence Richardson blandly agreed he told lies about the watch because he was frightened police might try to pin the murder on him. He had visited his aunt who had given him the watch to take to the repairers as it had a loose glass.

Captain Gurney, Chief Constable of the city decided that the case was strong enough to place Richardson before the courts and the public prosecutor who he consulted, agreed the circumstantial evidence justified proceedings. Richardson was committed to York Assizes.

Pleading not guilty in a firm voice when he appeared Richardson appeared unmoved by either the evidence against him, the admission by his own counsel that his story was full of holes or even when the Judge sternly rebuked him for taking his position too lightly. The jury returned a verdict of guilty on apparently overwhelming evidence and in the final electric moments

THE EAST HULL MURDER

Trial at York Assizes.

ACCUSED SENTENCED TO DEATH

in the court before sentence Mr. Justice Lawrence asked Richardson if he had anything to say. "All have to say is that I am innocent and that any punishment I receive will be an unjust punishment!" Richardson said calmly. So firm was his response that some jurors were seen to shift uncertainly in their seats but the Judge lost no time in passing the death sentence.

Because of military requirements at York Castle the condemned man was moved back to Hull for execution. He arrived at Hull Paragon Station accompanied by two war ders where a small crowd watched as he was walked a small van for conveyance to Hedon Road.

Still remaining calm throughout his last days Richardson received visits from his mother and from officers of the Salvation Army. He calmly wrote a request for a reprieve which read, "Grant me a reprieve that my life may be spared, not only for my own sake but for my dear wife's and my mother's who are so laid up on account of this sentence that has been passed upon me and more so that my true innocence of this crime may be brought to light which I am certain will be sooner or later." Amazingly he went to bed at ten o'clock on the night before his life was to end and slept soundly until 5.0 am. After a good breakfast he asked for writing materials and penned a short confession to the murder of his aunt and gave it to the Governor.

Just prior to the executioner entering his cell Richardson fell upon his knees and said quietly, "I confess my guilt and wish to go forth to my fellow men." With that the executioner Billington and his assistant entered and quickly pinioned his arms and led him the six steps into the execution chamber. A minute later it was done and one of the most vicious and callous murderers in Hull had gone calmly to his fate.

Had it not been for the last minute confession Richardson would have been just one more man judicially put to death in Britain without one shred of direct evidence against him and although local Hull newspapers wrote to Home Office asking for copies of this confession they were refused sight of it. A copy of the document is now reproduced and is the first occasion since Richardson's execution that it has been seen by the public.

SATURDAY, MARCH 29, 1902.

A VOICE FROM THE GRAVE.

Richardson's Last Letter.

PRISON COMMISSION
26 MAR 1902

A63252 / 27340.
26.3.02
17008
593

The following is the Confession of Arthur Richardson which he desired be made known to the lawful authorities.

"I, Arthur Richardson, did wilfully murder my Aunt Sarah Hebden, my motive in entering her house was not theft but murder. I trusted to chance to provide me with the weapon. I took nothing with me for the purpose. I entered her house at 7.30 on the morning of the murder & I remained there an hour & a half, leaving about 9 o'clock making my escape across the Groves Allotments. When I entered the house my Aunt & I had some words & in trying to avoid me, tripped over something & fell, in which attitude I struck her a blow. She then reached the tongs & knocked behind the fire grate to arouse the neighbours; I took the tongs from her & struck her with them on the head; she then arose & staggered towards the door behind which her body was found — whilst there & to silence her screams, for ahowed at the door frightened me & I struck her with the tongs until she died. The most horrible part of the murder forced was some words my Aunt uttered just as she was dying; taking my hand in both hers she said, 'I forgive you all Arthur', & then died — At the same moment I heard a voice close behind me which said audibly, 'Murder will out'. It was the voice of my conscience."

Signed H. C. Parkin.
Acting Chaplain.

March 25th 1902.
H.M. Prison Hull

Forwarded
W. R. Chidley
Governor

A63259/16

CERTIFICATE OF SURGEON.

31 Vic. Cap 24.

I, Edmund Henry Howlett the Surgeon of His Majesty's Prison of Kingston upon Hull hereby certify that I this day examined the Body of Arthur Richardson, on whom Judgment of Death was this day executed in the said Prison; and that on that Examination I found that the said Arthur Richardson was dead.

Dated this 25th day of March 1902

(Signature), E H Howlett

No. 279
(7599)

Another who was put out by the whole affair was the Under Sheriff of Hull — Arthur Rollitt who after the execution testily enquired of Home Office who was to pay the Executioner's fees. He was directed to read the Under Sheriff's Act and told that normally fees were £10 for an executioner £5 if it was cancelled at the last minute!

THE SLEEPING MURDERER

Jane Allen who lived at Andrew Marvell Terrace was to be described by the Judge at the trial of her murderer as "a woman of the unfortunate class!"

For most of the year 1902 this attractive young lady had been paid increasing attention by, amongst others, one William Bolton a 40-year old Second Engineer on a Hull steam trawler. Bolton was estranged from his wife and had become completely infatuated with Jane.

Jane Allen entertained a number of men at her house which was also occupied by a Mrs. Butterworth who was Jane's lodger.

Mrs. Bolton became aware of her husband's affair with Jane Allen and constantly visited the house at Andrew Marvell Terrace and badgered the occupants. Jane became very concerned by these disturbances and decided to stop associating with Bolton. In October 1902 she informed Mrs. Butterworth of her intention to marry one of her men 'friends', Charles Nicholson at Christmas. She said she did not wish to continue seeing Bolton.

On 17th October, shortly before 11.0 pm Bolton appeared at the house and Jane told Mrs. Butterworth not to let him come in. Bolton became highly incensed and insisted on entering the house. Despite Mrs. Butterworth's protestations he pushed past her and asked Jane why he could not see her. The girl told him she did not want to see him anymore as she was marrying Charlie.

At first angry, Bolton seemed to settle down when Mrs. Butterworth produced some stout. The three sat round the kitchen table quite amicably but Bolton was alternately raging and crying. At one stage he took a pin Jane had given him from his scarf and threw it in the fire saying, "You never are going to marry him!" Almost immediately he stopped raging and became maudlin saying, "Well if you do I hope you'll always be happy!"

He insisted on staying the night so Mrs. Butterworth agreed to sleep on the kitchen sofa and Jane and William Bolton retired to bed. Before going up Bolton asked her to call him between 6.0 and 7.0 am.

At 6.50 am she called him and afterwards heard Bolton and Jane laughing and joking together. She dozed off again only to be awakened by a noise at 8.30. She heard Jane cry "Oh dear, don't". The panic in the voice caused Mrs. Butterworth to hurry up to the bedroom and when she opened the door she was horrified to see the bed full of blood. She reached across and lifted Jane across Bolton and laid her on the floor. There were three gaping holes in the region of her heart but she was still alive! Bolton was on the bed holding a blood stained clasp knife in one hand and with a nasty wound in his own neck.

Mrs. Butterworth left the two and rushed to summon the police. Constables Barton and Burton arrived promptly with the police surgeon Dr. Lamb but it was too late for Jane Allen who had died of her wounds. As Bolton was taken from the house he said to Constable Burton, "I've done for Jenny, Charlie!"

William James Bolton was committed to stand trial for murder at York Assizes but already the Under Sheriff in Hull, William Hodgson, was having serious misgivings lest the accused man was sentenced to death and he had to attend an execution at Hull Prison. He wrote to Home Office suggesting it would be much simpler if Bolton was convicted, for the hanging to take place in York.

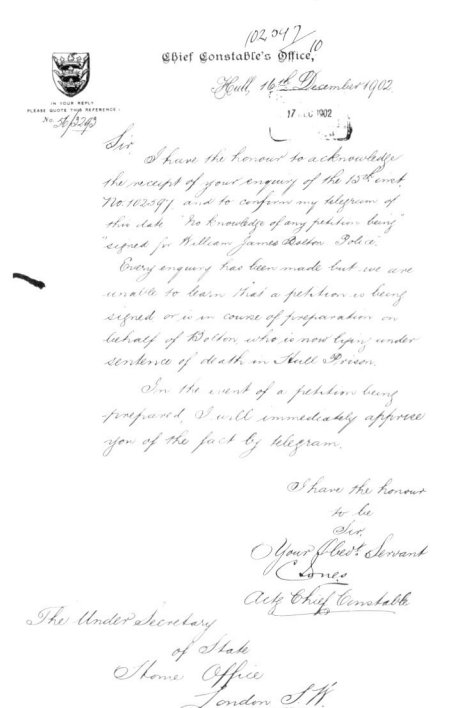

The Jury lost little time in finding Bolton guilty despite his advocate's most remarkable defence. He claimed that Bolton had committed the murder while semi-conscious in sleep and that there was therefore no element of premeditation!

As usual in murder cases, once the sentence

had been passed the Home Office made enquiries to establish whether or not a reprieve was justified. They wrote to the Judge who commented that he considered the verdict should have been Manslaughter on the grounds that there was no real premeditation. "Generally only premeditated murderers hang" his Lordship had replied.

Concerned about public opinion Home Office wrote to Hull's Chief Constable and enquired whether any petitions were likely in support of a reprieve. The laconic reply from the Chief was "No".

The execution was fixed for the day before Christmas Eve in 1902 at Hedon Road prison, Hull. Because of the representations by the Hull Under Sheriff the Home Office arranged for the Under Sheriff of York, Mr. Gray, to take charge of the hanging.

A contrite but cheerful Bolton spent his time in the condemned cell saying goodbye to his relatives and early on the morning of the 23rd December a large crowd, mostly women of the poorer class, gathered outside the main gate in Hedon Road to watch the comings and goings.

At 8.0 am the Billingham brothers William and John, entered the condemned cell and pinioned Bolton's arms and led him to the execution chamber. In a few moments the deed had been done. Another jealous man had met his just deserts.

102,59 2/6

DECLARATION OF SHERIFF
AND OTHERS.

31 Vict. Cap. 24.

We, the undersigned, hereby declare that Judgment of Death was this Day executed on *William James Bolton* in His Majesty's Prison of *Kingston-upon-Hull* in our presence.

Dated this 23rd day of *December 1902*.

Edwin Gray Under Sheriff of *Yorkshire*.

J W Morrill Justice of the Peace for *the City and County of Kingston-upon-Hull*

W R Cheedey Governor of the said Prison.

J B S Watson Chaplain of the said Prison.

No. 280

MURDER AT SCAMPSTON

Mr. and Mrs. Brewster were farmers at Grange Farm, Scampston and employed both Annie Marshall, a 16-year old girl from Lissett as house servant and 20-years old Charles William Ashton as a 'third lad'.

On a warm and sunny Sunday evening in September 1903 Annie left the house to make her weekly visit to the local church and sometime later Ashton also left the house. The evening wore on and the Brewsters retired to bed expecting the servants to return in due course. Next morning, to their dismay, Annie Marshall was missing. The police were informed and a search commenced.

The local constable, Charles Broughton was a 39-years old and had thirteen years police service to his credit. Never having felt such a feeling of foreboding about a case before, he questioned all the servants and Ashton mentioned he had seen poachers on the land the previous evening and he produced a hat identified as Annie's which he said he had found in the wood. The constable who lived at Rillington and knew the area well was surprised the hat was soaking wet whereas Ashton claimed to have found it on dry ground. Suspicious, the policeman decided to take Ashton with him to establish where the poachers had been seen.

When Ashton indicated the spot the constable could see no sign of people having been in the undergrowth and his suspicions increased. Ashton then made the odd statement that he felt Annie would have been thrown from a bridge into the river. Even more puzzled by this, the constable allowed himself to be guided along the river bank until all of a sudden Ashton exclaimed, "There she is". To the constable the object Ashton was excitedly pointing to looked like an old carpet bag. But, sure enough it was the body of Annie Marshall. The girl had been assaulted, suffocated by having grass stuffed into her mouth and finally shot.

Broughton decided this was all too much of a coincidence and he immediately arrested Ashton on suspicion of murder and informed Superintendent Johnson. Ashton's room at the farm was searched and in his box was found bloodstained clothing and a revolver. He

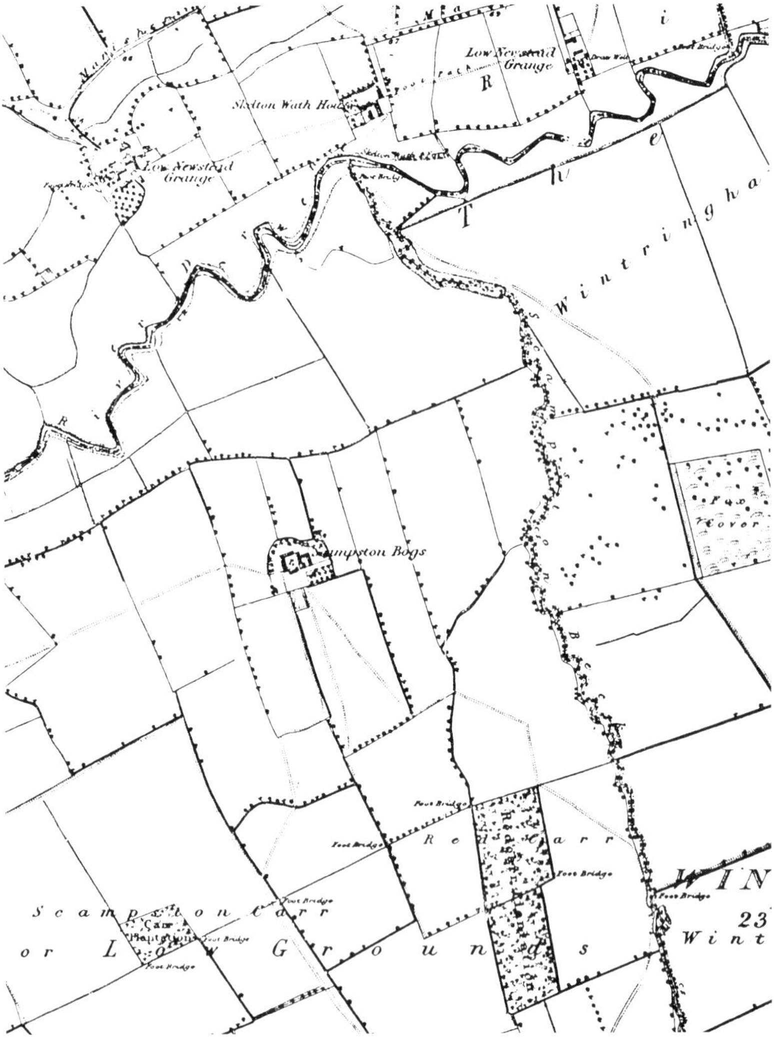
Low Newstead Grange
Skelton Wath House
Low Newstead Grange
Wintringham
Scampton Bogs
Fox Cover
Foot Bridge
Foot Bridge
Foot Bridge
Foot Bridge
Foot Bridge
Foot Bridge
Foot Bridge
Red Carr
Scampton Carr
or Low Grounds
Car Plantation
Wint
23

Grange Farm, Scampston.

also had a purse which he claimed to have been his grandmothers but which was identified as Annies. Later, the Superintendent questioned Ashton at the police station and he confessed to murdering the girl.

Mr. Luke White MP, the coroner, decided to hold the Inquest at Grange Farm and Ashton was brought from Norton police station to be present. Every village en route was crowded with people trying to glimpse the prisoner and many waited at the farm entrance to see him. Deciding the farm rooms were too small Mr. White elected to have the inquest on the lawn. After hearing the evidence the jury returned a verdict of wilful murder and the Coroner committed Ashton for trial at York. He was taken back to Norton to appear formally before the Justices there and was remanded to Hull prison.

When he returned for the committal at Norton some days later the excitement was intense throughout the county. As he travelled by train from Hull crowds gathered on platforms of every station where the train stopped and stared at the hapless prisoner. At Driffield the Malton train stood waiting and police had to force a way for the warders and their prisoner through the jostling crowds. The journey was completed with drawn blinds. A crowded bench of curious magistrates at Norton finally committed the young man to York.

Subsequently convicted and sentenced to death, the case moved to consideration by Home Office whether a reprieve should be granted. As usual the trial judge was consulted but he reported that it "was a very bad murder indeed". The only consideration which exercised the minds of Home Office officials was the comparative youth of the murderer. However a firm minute on the file by the then Under Secretary reads, "In case of prisoners aged 18, 19, and 20 recommendations on the grounds of age have been repeatedly disregarded if murder was a bad one."

The die was cast and Ashton was hanged at Hull prison on 22nd December 1903. At the meeting of the Standing Joint Committee in January 1904. Charles Broughton, by now acting sergeant, was granted a merit badge with extra pay for the intelligence and promptitude which he showed in dealing with the case. The chairman said that had it not been for his 'tact' (*sic*) the murder might have remained undiscovered for a considerable time and facilities could then have been afforded for the guilty man to have escaped.

BLACK TUESDAYS

It was March 1908, the start of yet another Edwardian 'season' when aristocratic society dressed in the height of fashion and spent their time living luxuriously between houses in London and the country and sometimes moving to the warmth of the south of France. In the north eastern fishing port of Hull, Gertrude Siddle was in her early twenties and already had two young children when she decided to leave her ne'er-do-well husband Thomas. Although a competent bricklayer he persistently failed to support his wife and young family. Fond of drink and the company of other men Thomas seldom gave his wife any of his wages despite her pleas. In desperation she pawned her wedding ring for five shillings but learning of this Thomas took the pawn ticket from her and sold it in a pub for eighteen pence. Ultimately with children hungry and in threadbare clothes Gertrude reached the end of her tether.

Obtaining lodgings with friendly Mrs. Felcey in Tyne Street, Gertrude applied for separation and maintenance orders which the Hull Magistates had no hesitation in granting. Still little or no money was forthcoming from Siddle who stubbornly refused to comply with the court order. The inevitable happened and the Magistrates issued a committal warrant ordering that Thomas Siddle should go to prison for 30 days on 10th June unless he paid his maintenance arrears.

On Tuesday 9th June, Siddle called to see his wife and children at Tyne Street. Despite smelling strongly of drink he appeared calm so Mrs. Felcey allowed him in and was present when he saw his wife. Thomas apologised to Gertrude for not paying her but said she looked so comfortable he didn't think she needed it! How did he know she was not being supported by another man? His tone changed when he hissed "You will never have another man while I'm alive!" "I'm not frightened of you", replied Gertrude, "but there isn't any other man".

Appearing to calm down Siddle indicated he was leaving and he walked to Gertrude and shook hands. He turned and put his hand in his pocket and suddenly produced a razor and before either woman could move he had slashed Gertrude across the throat two or three times. Both women screamed and Gertrude crashed to the floor with blood pumping from her neck. Siddle turned, pushed past a distracted Mrs. Felcey and left the house.

Gertrude Siddle died within the hour and police were notified and Siddle was soon arrested in a city centre public house. On Tuesday 14th July he appeared before Mr. Justice Grantham at York Assizes charged with murdering his wife. He pleaded not guilty.

Siddle's defence was not a denial that he had killed his wife but that he had not known what he was doing at the time. He claimed his mind had blanked out after shaking her hands until he found himself in the street with blood on his knees. The case was concluded with the Judge telling the Jury he could see no reason why a manslaughter verdict should be returned and emphasising that drink was no excuse for crime. After a retirement of just five minutes the Jury returned and announced a guilty verdict.

Sentenced to death Siddle began possibly the most macabre part of the ritual for condemned men. Most of the onlookers in the court waited to see him march across the courtyard at York Castle to his cell. Next day a crowded platform at York railway station saw him walked between two warders to the 7.0 am train for Hull. When he eventually got to the reserved first class compartment the prison warders pulled down the blinds so the morbid onlookers turned their attention to the next but one compartment where Siddle's father was talking out of the window to the weeping figure of Siddle's aunt.

On arrival at Hull Paragon station, the two warders assisted by railway police, had to force a way through a large crowd anxious to see the condemned man. Although mostly sympathetic there were cries of 'Hang the murderer' as Siddle, wearing a sickly smile was piled into a cab. Whipping up the horse the cabbie trotted out of the station chased by a shouting mob of young men and boys.

Siddle was housed in the condemned cell at Hedon Road prison and the execution was fixed for 4th August, the day after August Bank Holiday Monday. He was visited by his family including on one poignant occasion by his small children. Their constant chatter was too much for Siddle and the adults accompanying them and the visit ended with everyone in tears. The Tuesday prior to the day fixed for the execution saw Sculcoates' Board of Visitors considering a letter from Siddle asking that dock labourer Mr.

<u>Copy of Letter written by Thomas Sidde, (6672).</u>

Hull, Prison
30th July, 1908.

Dear Aunt uncle I now take the pleasure of writeing to you hopeing to find you in good health has it leaves me at present cheer up and dont fret about me as I'm not worthy of it. I ham verry sorry to bring this disgrace on our faimley and I hope and trust in god I ham the last one of them to meat this awful end I acknowledge my deed which I deeply regret and I hope the lord will forgive me for it I did not now whatever I was doing at that time I was muttled in drink and had been fore some time and the people where she was liveing at caused all the truble we were happy and comfortable wile they got her away but it had been going on along wile unknown to me and when I was paying her money they would interfere with me it was not the money they wanted they wanted me in gaol so I could not see them I so myself that things was going wrong with them so I said I would not Pay no more but I would keep my children but I will forgive all my enemies for all the wrong they have done to me I ham longing to see my children god help them what a disgrace it will be fore them when they grow up to now their ~~murdered~~ Mother murdered and the farther hanged god have mercy on the two of our souls I have just read in the bible. For God hath not appointed us to wrath but to obtain salvation by our Lord Jesus

Christ how I little knew of the bible when I was free
or I would have read it more of it I hope my
little ones will know more about it since I rote the
above I have seen the 4 children and kissed them
for the last thime on earth god help them they
wanted to come to me bless them thank god now
I can die in Peace X Dear Susan and Jack I give my
best love to you hopeing that you will foregive me
for this awful sin and also cussin Lizzy and her
husband and his brother and dont let no one know
I ham yours coussin Look what a disgrace it will
be to you all but it cant be help now I wish
it could. Think of me kindly when I ham gon
as I ham thinking of all friends to the hour of my
Death which it wont be long now I wound like to
tell you the cause of my possition drink Jelsey and
bad temper they are the worst faults a man can have
and I had them. has I could not help them faults
I wounder if god will alow for them I hope So
also hoping for his mercy as I want it with kind
love to you all from your Loveing and regreting relation

            Thomas Siddle
   God Bless you all good bye.

Please write back as soone as you can

16779/

HOME OFFICE
RECEIVED
3 AUG 1908

H. M. Prison, Hull
1st Aug 1908

Re Thomas Siddle
Under sentence of death

Sir,

I have the honour to acknowledge the receipt of your communication of yesterday (No 167.791) that the Secretary of State having had under his consideration the case of the above named, has failed to discover any sufficient grounds to justify him in advising His Majesty to interfere with the due course of law.

I beg to confirm my telegram of to-day acknowledging receipt of the communication and stating that the sentence will therefore be carried out on Tuesday next.

I have the honour to be
Sir
Your Obedient Servant
M Sumner
Chief W. in charge

The Under Secretary
of State
Home Office
Whitehall
SW

No. 344
(7344)

Coggan and his wife might have his youngest child, Harry, to bring up as their own. His letter to Mr. and Mrs. Coggan read,

> *"Dear friends, I write you hoping you are well as it leaves me. Thank you very much for the kindness you have afforded me. I wish very much for you to have little Harry. I know you will be father and mother to him and will bring him up as one of your own."*

The Board unanimously acceded to the application.

Efforts to seek a reprieve were ended by a letter from the Home Secretary to Siddle's father in which he said he could find no grounds on which he could recommend the King to intervene. This final blow seemed to affect Siddle very badly and he began to deteriorate seriously. He didn't sleep and had to be washed and fed by the warders who were with him day and night.

At 8.30 am on Tuesday 4th August, Albert Pierrepoint viewed the prisoner and made his preparations and at a few minutes before 9.0 am he, together with the Governor, the Chaplain, the Under Sheriff and some warders, entered the cell. Siddle was pinioned and marched to the drop. At 9.0 am exactly Pierrepoint pulled the lever and Siddle was dead. The public executioner hurried out of the prison to make for Durham where he had another execution to perform that morning!

The day after the execution the *Hull News* pointed out the significance of Tuesdays in the events. It was Tuesday on which the murder was committed, a Tuesday Siddle was sentenced to death and another Tuesday when he went to meet his maker.

THE DEATH PENALTY.

Execution of Siddle in Hull Gaol.

DEATH ON A WITHERNSEA BEACH

At nine o'clock on a September Sunday morning in 1908, Superintendent Maw had hardly finished his breakfast when he heard a knock on his door at Withernsea Police Station. On opening it he was surprised to find an excited crowd. He was even more taken aback when a man nearest to him declared calmly, "I want you to take me in charge!" "Oh, why's that?" asked the superintendent. Before the man could reply a voice from the crowd called, "Oh he has killed a woman on the sands — it's alright there is a dead body. That's why he wants to be taken in charge!"

Concealing his surprise and establishing the man was 22-year old Charles Henry Woodman, from Hull, the superintendent locked him in a cell and, accompanied by the jostling crowd, made his way to the beach. On arrival a small boy handed him a knife with what appeared to be blood stains on it and pointed to the body of a teenaged girl. Arranging for the police photographer to attend the superintendent tried to prevent the crowd trampling over the evidence. His efforts were in vain however and crowds of locals and trippers scrambled everywhere, one particularly morbid individual collecting bloodstained sand in a child's bucket!

Superintendent Maw later tried to question Woodman but found he had gone into his shell and refused to answer. In the end he contented himself by telling the prisoner he would be charged with the murder of an unknown woman. Curiously he then allowed the prisoner to wash blood stains from his hands.

Enquiries soon revealed the deceased to be 21-year old Kate Lee of 41 Edgar street, Hull who had been working as a barmaid at the Queen's Hotel, Withernsea. Woodman himself turned out to be a popular member of the staff at Liverpool Street tramway sheds, in Hull who had become infatuated with Lee and had visited her at Withernsea the Friday prior to the body being found. He stayed the weekend and was apparently very jealous when he saw Kate in company with another man. He had taken her to the beach and murdered her by cutting her throat sometime on Saturday night.

In November Woodman appeared at York Assizes charged with the murder where it was revealed his father spent 20 years in an asylum. He himself was declared unfit to plead and was ordered to be detained indefinitely in a secure place.

THE MOLESCROFT MURDER

There is a grave in St. John's Cemetery, Queensgate, Beverley on which the tombstone records that John Henry Tindale who died aged 52 on 18th November 1919 and his wife Minnie who died on 31st August 1950 are buried there. Sadly there is no mention of their youngest daughter Lily who was the first to be buried in this family grave in 1917. The procession of her white flower covered coffin to the cemetery had been watched by large crowds.

The Tindale family had three daughters and were originally from Routh on the Beverley to Bridlington Road. They were living at Constitution Hill Farm about 1½ miles outside Beverley on the Malton Road in 1917. John Tindale was the foreman at the farm.

Lily was a well developed, pretty dark haired girl of 13 years who had attended St. Mary's Girl's School in Beverley until she was 12. She was part of an affectionate, hard-working and well respected family.

The Great War was at its height on the 15th February and the family were at their normal daily tasks when about 1.30 pm Lily brought some firewood she had been chopping, into the house. She went back out to the stackyard and that was the last time she was seen alive. At about 3 o'clock Mrs. Tindale wondered what had happened to Lily and on not finding her she raised the alarm. She called Gertrude another daughter who also made an abortive search of the farm and the by now thoroughly alarmed woman sent for her husband. At about 4.0 pm he started a search, concentrating on the stackyard.

Suddenly something caught his eye beneath the straw. He was later to describe what happened next. "What I saw there horrified me. There were splashes of blood about and under a heap of loose straw between two stacks I found the body of my poor girl, her throat shockingly cut and her clothing covered in blood and dirt."

Police were later to confirm that the lower part of the girl's body was naked and massively blood stained. Yet there was no sign that she had been sexually molested.

Dr. Munro, summoned to the scene pronounced death and spoke

THE BEVERLEY MURDER.

FUNERAL OF THE VICTIM.

A PATHETIC SCENE.

[BY OUR OWN REPORTER.]

A pathetic scene, such as has seldom been witnessed in Beverley, was the funeral last Monday afternoon of Lily Tindale, the victim of the diabolical murder which was perpetrated the previous Thursday at the lonely farm on Constitution Hill, known as Constitution Farm at Molescroft.

The crime has caused a thrill of horror in all parts, not only of the East Riding, but of this country, and a crowd of several hundreds of public sympathisers gathered at the funeral.

The cortege left the farm where the little girl was so cruelly done to her death in the early afternoon, and it was a sad and mournful procession from Constitution Hill to Keldgate to St. John's Cemetery, where the interment took place amidst every manifestation of sorrow.

The coffin was of wood, covered with embossed swan's down, pure white in colour, with brass furniture, and there was a fringe of white looping round the edges. On the coffin was a little brass plate inscribed:

Lily Tindale,
Died February 15th, 1917,
Aged 13 years 11 months.

Surmounting the coffin was a number of wreaths, sent by the following:—Father and mother, Mr Hanson and family, the workmen, Bob, Herbert and Edith (cousins), from her cousin Gerty, Harold and Tom Walker, Mr and Mrs C. Walker, Laura, Harold and Tom Walker, Mr and Mrs C. Meadley, Frank, Mr and Mrs Woods (Beverley Parks), teachers and older scholars of St Mary's Girls' School, Mary Boutell, J. and Amos Thompson and family, and others.

The interment took place at St. John's Cemetery, which is governed by the Joint Burial Board for the parish of St. John which comprises the township of Molescroft.

The father, mother, and other relatives were present, and also Mr J. W. Hanson, tenant of the farm.

The Rev W. E. Wigfall, perpetual curate of Beverley Minster, conducted the funeral service.

The undertaker was Mr. J. R. Foley, of Toll Gavel.

of an obvious struggle put up by Lily who in addition to having her throat cut from 'ear to ear' also had a badly blackened left eye.

When the body was moved, part of a razor was found on the straw as was a partly chewed plug of tobacco.

Four workers at the farm lived in the farm house as lodgers and when a check was made it was discovered that one of them, a shepherd named John William Thompson and commonly called Jack was missing. Forty-three years old bachelor Thompson was a native of Beverley and had worked on the farm for a year. Unusually he had failed to come in for dinner when summoned that day. Elsie Tindale, one of Lily's elder sisters had seen him walking towards the Molescroft pub at about 12.20 pm as she was returning home from her work in Beverley. An hour later she had been looking out of her bedroom window and had seen Thompson walking towards the stackyard at the farm. This was about the time that Lily had last been seen alive.

Police enquiries at the Molescroft pub discovered that Thompson had been there and had been served with two pints of beer and a plug of tobacco. He had left at about 1.0 pm.

Suspicion now fairly centred on Thompson and Beverley Borough police were asked to make enquiries to find him as he had relatives in the town. In view of the serious nature of the case the chief constable of the small force called off-duty detectives from their homes to help in the hunt. Detectives were quite used to being disturbed at home and Constable James Bayley was called from his house in Gilbert Lane and sent to check the public houses in town. He visited a public house in Walkergate at about five minutes past six and immediately saw a man he thought was the suspect who was described as being under-sized, with sallow complexion and a moustache. Thompson admitted his identity and when told he was being arrested he said nothing. When the officer took hold of his arm however he snarled, "What the ----- is the game?"

Taken to Beverley Police Station it was noticed his hands and clothing were heavily bloodstained. He showed what was later to be described as a "callous indifference" to his situation and asked if he could light his pipe. The clay pipe he produced was also heavily bloodstained.

The County officers arrived to collect him and he was removed to their station. Made to undress it was found that blood had stained his knees, fingers and most of his clothing. He was charged with

Lily's murder, placed before Magistrates and taken by train from Beverley to Hull and then by cab to Hedon Road prison.

Police continued to look for evidence at and near to the murder scene and next day Sergeant Jackson noted unusually patterned boot marks near to where the body had lain which matched those worn by Thompson. He followed the marks made by the boots through a hedge and into a field bordering the Leconfield road. Under some grass and dead leaves in the hedge bottom he found a razor case and part of a razor. These were later identified as Thompson's.

When he next appeared at the Magistrates' Court Thompson was questioned by Deputy Chief Constable Crisp at Sessions House and made a statement in which he claimed the blood found everywhere had been the result of bleeding a sheep. He also admitted putting the razor in the hedgerow.

Unfortunately for Thompson Mr. Tindale was able to say that no sheep had been bled by or in the presence of Thompson and the County Analyst proved the blood was human.

When the case appeared at York Assizes on 9th March 1919, Mr. E. Short K.C., M.P., appeared for the Prosecution but Thompson was not represented. The Judge, Mr. Justice McArdie asked a Mr. C. Paley Scott to represent the prisoner. He decided to admit the facts but to put forward a defence of insanity. It seemed to have little effect on the Jury who took a short nineteen minutes to return a verdict of 'Guilty'.

Thompson who had maintained an attitude of stolid indifference throughout the case when asked by the Judge if he had anything to

THE EAST RIDING FARM MURDER.

SHEPHERD SENTENCED TO DEATH

say replied "Nothing, Sir." Sentenced to death Thompson was removed to Armley Prison in Leeds.

At 9.0 am on the 27th March, a mere sixteen days after being sentenced and only just over a month after the murder itself, executioners J. W. Pierrepoint and his assistant W. Willis entered the condemned cell and pinioned the arms of an unresisting and almost disinterested Thompson who then walked calmly into the execution chamber and was hanged.

BEVERLEY MURDERER EXECUTED.

SAID TO HAVE MADE A CONFESSION.

A DRUMMER BOY'S ESCAPE FROM THE HANGMAN

The City of Kingston-upon-Hull was the scene of an impressive and sombre funeral on Monday the 8th October 1923. A horse-drawn gun carriage surrounded by marching troops with rifles reversed in mourning; a coffin covered by the Union flag and carried by a bareheaded guard-of-honour; a large crowd of military and civilian mourners — it was obviously a person of some eminence being buried. In fact the body being ceremoniously laid to rest was that of 17-year old drummer boy James Frederick Ellis of the 1st Leicestershire Regiment whose home was Alpha Terrace, Nornabell Street, one of the hundreds of similar nondescript dwellings in the City after the Great War. Ellis had been missing, presumed absent without leave from his regiment in Aldershot since May the same year when his bleached skeleton had been discovered four months later under a blackberry bush near a wild area known as Long Valley just outside Aldershot.

In the funeral procession and supported by two friends but bravely erect, walked the figure of ex Regimental Sergeant Major Dearnley who lived across the street from the Ellis family. His son, Lance Corporal Albert Edward Dearnley, the bosom pal of Ellis and who had joined the Army with him, was currently remanded in custody charged with his friend's murder!

When the decomposed body of Ellis was found the head was covered with an army overcoat tightly bound by an army webbing belt. The arms and legs were tied together at the back of the body with a long length of drum rope. The world famous Pathologist, Sir Bernard Spilsbury examined the body and soon discovered it had been subjected to extreme violence with two ribs and two vertebrae fractured and part of the breast bone completely detached from the rib cage. There seemed no doubt — it was murder!

Superintendent Davies of Aldershot leading the enquiry soon decided the dead man's friend — Albert Dearnley, must be a good suspect and arrested him.

Dearnley's story was that he and Ellis had decided to desert from the Army in May and that Ellis had wanted to go first to Hull, get

The military cortège carrying the body of Drummer Ellis through Hull.

Drummer Ellis's coffin.

Drummer Ellis.

some money by hook or crook and then take a passage to America. A drummer sergeant in the regiment was Sergeant Ormes whose sister-in-law Hilda Storey had become Dearnley's girlfriend. Dearnley said Ellis was jealous of his friendship with Hilda to such a degree that he had insulted her at a dance by calling her an 'old cow'. On the day Ellis disappeared from the Regiment the two young soldiers had gone for a drink and then for a walk on the outskirts of Aldershot army camp. Being slightly merry they decided to play Cowboys and Indians. Dearnley lassoed Ellis who challenged him to tie him up. He did so

Ex RSM Dearnley supported by friends at Drummer Ellis's funeral.

and Ellis boasted that he would escape and follow him back to camp. When he didn't appear he assumed his friend had carried out his threat to desert.

Not surprisingly the police didn't believe him and Lance Corporal Dearnley was committed for trial and appeared before

IDENTIFIED BY TEETH.

INQUEST OPENED ON BODY OF DRUMMER ELLIS.

BONES BLEACHED WHITE BY WEATHER.

Mr. Justice Avory at Hampshire Assizes in November 1923. He pleaded not guilty to murder but guilty to manslaughter on the grounds that he had no intention to kill Ellis but accepted that leaving him bound and gagged had been a reckless thing to do. The Jury decided he was guilty of murder and on 27th November the Judge donned the black cap and sentenced him to death. The execution was fixed for the 18th December which was a Tuesday, the normal day for executions.

Dearnley's lawyers advised an appeal and one was duly lodged. Local people in Hull also signed a massive petition asking that the young man's life be spared. Home Office consulted the trial Judge who replied by saying he entirely agreed with the Jury's verdict and that the prisoner's demeanour "had been callous throughout the trial". Officials considering the case noted that Dearnley's brother was in a mental asylum and his mother had also been in one for a few months in 1907. They agreed with the Judge that the evidence was compelling and as far as the petition from Hull was concerned this was dismissed as being simply a 'plea for a life to be spared'. On Thursday 4th January it was announced that the appeal would be dismissed and the new date for execution was to be 8th January 1924 at 9.0 am.

Hull was on tenterhooks. Renewed efforts were made to have the lad reprieved. Only four days remained before the young Hull soldier would walk the few yards from the condemned cell in Winchester Prison into the execution chamber and be hanged by the Public Executioner. They knew that once the weekend prior to an execution date had been reached there was no hope of saving a person from the hangman!

Mr. and Mrs. Dearnley made the sad journey by train to Winchester and were allowed to see Albert. On the morning prior to the execution Mrs. Dearnley rcalled the traumatic last visit they

No. in Register 452558

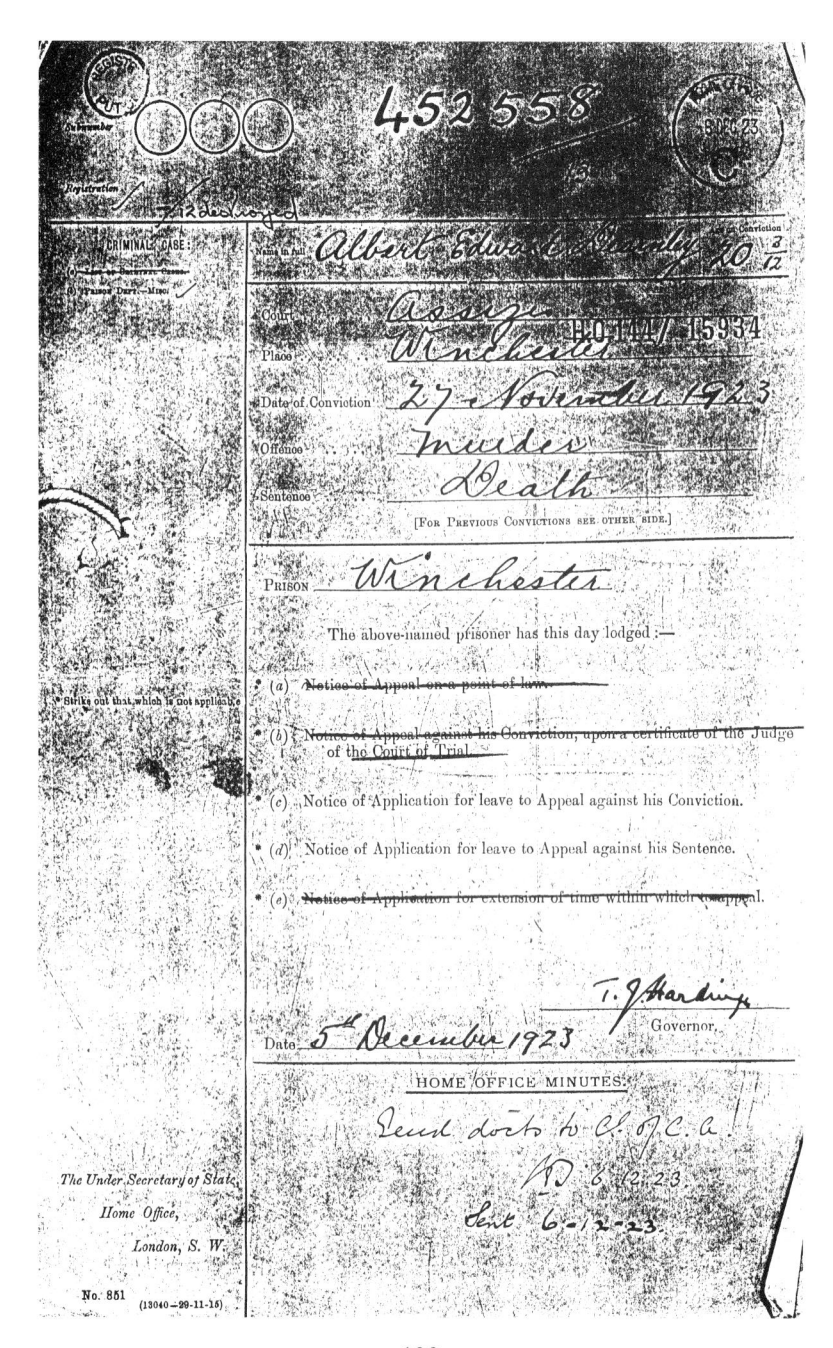

Registration _____

CRIMINAL CASE

Name in full: Albert Edward *[Bradley]* 20   3/12 Conviction

Court: Assize
Place: Winchester

Date of Conviction: 27 November 1923

Offence: Murder

Sentence: Death

[FOR PREVIOUS CONVICTIONS SEE OTHER SIDE.]

PRISON: Winchester

The above-named prisoner has this day lodged:—

Strike out that which is not applicable

* (a) ~~Notice of Appeal on a point of law.~~

* (b) ~~Notice of Appeal against his Conviction, upon a certificate of the Judge of the Court of Trial.~~

* (c) Notice of Application for leave to Appeal against his Conviction.

* (d) Notice of Application for leave to Appeal against his Sentence.

* (e) ~~Notice of Application for extension of time within which to appeal.~~

Date 5th December 1923

T. J. Harding
Governor.

HOME OFFICE MINUTES:

Send docts to C. of C.A.
ND 6/12/23
Sent 6-12-23

The Under Secretary of State,
Home Office,
London, S.W.

No. 851   (13040—29-11-15)

were allowed. They entered the prison at two minutes to eight and left again at fifteen minutes past the hour. They were not allowed to touch Albert who sat between two warders ten feet away from them. They returned home with feelings completely numbed and on arrival went straight to Albert's grandparent's house to give them their grandsons's last message.

On entering the house they were astonished to find it full of noise and they themselves were immediately hugged by excited and smiling relatives — their son had been reprieved at the very last minute — they couldn't believe it. It was a dramatic development at a later stage than ever before seen in British legal history.

But why? What had transpired to change the Home Secretary's mind? The official announcement merely said that as a result of additional evidence provided by the condemned man, the sentence had been commuted to penal servitude for life. Hull was agog with excitement and rumour — what was the additional evidence?

No-one ever discovered the true story, and it was not until over seventy years after the event, that this writer was able to breach Home Office secrecy and establish the true facts surrounding Albert Dearnley's dramatic reprieve. This is what happened.

The execution was fixed and the hangman had been booked. Everything was going normally until, with only three days to live the condemned man wrote a last letter to his sweetheart Hilda Storey. In the letter he said he had not told the truth at the trial because to have

DEARNLEY'S RAY OF HOPE.

FRESH INFORMATION CAUSES POST-PONEMENT OF EXECUTION.

IS SOME OTHER PERSON INVOLVED?

HOW OVERJOYED PARENTS RECEIVED THE NEWS.

done so would have brought shame on himself and on his family. As usual with correspondence to and from condemned prisoners, the Governor of the prison had to censor it.

Very conscious of the dreadful finality of an execution the Governor went to the condemned cell and, dismissing the two warders, sat with Dearnley and questioned him about the contents of the letter. Eventually and after much coaxing the story came out.

Soon after going to Aldershot Dearnley had been made a servant to the Drummer Sergeant — Sergeant Ormes. It had not been long before the Sergeant had seduced the young man and regular homosexual practices took place between them. On one occasion they were caught in the act by Drummer Ellis. Ellis had then insisted that Dearnley become his lover too or he would inform the authorities of what he had seen. Dearnley accepted this but when he became friendly with Hilda, Ellis became extremely jealous and threatened to tell her of their own relationship and of Dearnley's affair with her own brother-in-law. It had been as a result of Ellis's blackmail that in the end he had lost his temper and killed him. Since it had happened, even though his own life had become forfeit, he had been unable to admit the truth because of the shame it would have brought on him and his family.

As soon as he got this story the Prison Governor realised there was no time to lose and he contacted Home Office. The Prison doctor examined Dearnley and said the signs on the young man's body confirmed his story. Home Office contacted the military to locate Sergeant Orme and on the 7th January, the day before the execution was due, the Sergeant was brought to London and interviewed by a representative of the Public Prosecutor's Office. Homosexual activity, even in private, was illegal and a serious offence but, in view of the urgency, Ormes was told that if he told the truth, even if it incriminated him, he would not be prosecuted. After much prevarication the Sergeant admitted Dearnley's story about their homosexual activities was true.

Frantic efforts were made to contact the Home Secretary Lord Bridgeman, who was somewhere in his home County of Shropshire and urgent messages were sent asking him to contact London. When he was at last located hasty consultations were held and he agreed the additional evidence could have been sufficient to sway the Jury at Dearnley's trial in favour of a Manslaughter verdict so he halted the execution. The Prison Governor was informed and the hangman who had already secretly viewed the condemned man to estimate his weight, was stood down.

Dearnley was reprieved to the relief and mystification of his friends and the whole population of his home City. The secret which he would rather have hanged for than reveal was faithfully kept by his country until well after he had been forgotten.

THE LINCOLNSHIRE MURDERESS

Things were not all they should have been at No. 20 Council Houses, Kirby-on-Bain, in Lincolnshire in 1934. Arthur Major and his wife Ethel Lily had been married since 1918 but she alleged the marriage was unhappy, that he was addicted to drink and constantly assaulted her. This despite the fact that Arthur was a well respected long distance lorry driver and sidesman at the local church.

Perhaps more to the point was Ethel's belief that her husband was having an affair with a neighbour, Mrs. Kettleborough. Certainly the marital relationship had deteriorated to such an extent that by May 1934 the two were separately buying and eating their own food.

On the 22nd May Arthur put some corned beef on his shelf in the pantry and later ate some for tea. Almost immediately he started frothing at the mouth and his body began twitching uncontrollably. Although he was obviously very ill his wife failed to notify the doctor until 10.0 pm the same day.

Next morning a neighbour noticed Ethel scraping something from a plate which two dogs belonging to the neighbour immediately ate. Within seconds the dogs had fallen to the ground and become completely stiff. They died. Later the same day Mrs. Major instructed her son to burn some shelf paper on which her husband's corned beef had been standing.

Her husband was still very sick and, obviously informed by the suspicious neighbour Mrs. Kettlebrough, the local police sergeant called round. When he enquired after her husband's health Mrs. Major said he had epileptic fits and was experiencing one at the time. The sergeant later recalled she also rather strangely said, "but he will not get better and drive that lorry again!"

Despite this prediction her husband's condition showed signs of improvement on the 24th May but this was short lived and he died that same evening. Ethel Major visited the doctor and told him the news and was issued with a death certificate giving cause of death as Epilepsy.

The Village of Kirby-on-Bain scene of the murder by Ethel Major.

While she was making the funeral arrangements the police sergeant again called and was greeted by Ethel with the words, "Why have you come? I'm not under suspicion am I?"

Arrangements were made to exhume the neighbour's two dogs and the autopsy revealed they had been poisoned with strychnine. The funeral of Arthur Major was halted and a post mortem held which revealed that he too had died from the poison. The Chief Constable of Lincolnshire decided the case was too complicated for his officers to handle and called in detectives from Scotland Yard.

The two London detectives immediately tackled Ethel who denied all responsibility and blamed the corned beef which she said had appeared to be black before her husband had eaten it. "In any case I didn't have any strychnine" she said. Quietly the detective said, "But Mrs. Major, I haven't mentioned strychnine!" "I'm sorry, I made a mistake," stammered the woman. "Did you send your son to buy any corned beef?" the detective continued. "No," and with her voice rising Ethel went on strangely, "and if any woman in the village says I did she's a liar! they're all liars!" The policeman called Mrs. Major's son into the room and said, "Did your mother send you to buy some corned beef?" "Yes she did! — don't you remember Mum?" was the lad's innocent reply.

Ethel's father was a gamekeeper and a new key found in her purse fitted the cupboard where he kept poison including strychnine for use in his job. The investigating officers took her to her father's house and showed her how the key fitted and asked how she had come to be with it. Immediately Ethel shouted, "yes he was poisoned — it was that Mrs. Kettleborough!"

The evidence against her eventually being overwhelming Ethel Major was charged with murder and appeared before the November Assizes at Lincoln. Mr. O'Sullivan appeared for the Crown and a young Norman Birkett KC defended Ethel Major. The Jury had no hesitation in finding her guilty of murder and the Judge donned his black cap and sentenced her to death.

The condemned woman was removed to Hull Prison for execution and placed in the condemned cell. Appeals were made to no avail and the final date for execution was fixed for the 19th December — just five days before Christmas 1934.

All memories of the dreadful murder were forgotten in Hull and one thing only was in the minds of people in and around the prison. Someone, a woman, was to be executed nearby and just before Christmas! Some declared it quite put them off preparing for the festive season. The Lord Mayor, Alderman Stark, took up the cause and arranged for Home Office and The King to be petitioned. No-one really thought the execution could go ahead —surely it would be stopped and a reprieve granted.

The night prior to the execution arrived and Pierrepoint the hangman was at the prison with his assistant. Frantic last minute efforts were made to stop the dreadful event, the Lord Mayor stayed up all night telegraphing London but slowly a crowd began to collect in macabre anticipation as morning arrived.

Inside the prison the condemned woman was in a state of complete collapse and a doctor had been present with her all night. Still the preparations went ahead and the crowd grew. Two minutes to 9.0 am and Mrs. Ethel Lily Major was carried into the execution chamber and supported while the hangman quickly pinioned her arms and slipped the noose around her neck. The people with her stepped away and the fatal trap opened to receive

Mrs. Ethel Major.

Mr. Justice Charles who passed the death sentence Mrs. Ethel Major.

the last shrieking movements of her body.

Ethel Major had the double privilege of being the last person to be hanged in Hull Gaol and her ghost is still said to walk the corridors. Staff and inmates claim she has been seen and heard weeping and it is claimed there are some inmates who will not go to bed in the gaol unless they have a bible under their pillow!

LORD MAYOR'S TELEGRAM TO HOME SECRETARY

"FOR SAKE OF HUMANITY .. THIS SEASON OF GOOD WILL"

SON OF A POLICE INSPECTOR

It was about a quarter to ten on a Summer's evening with the light just beginning to fade when Inspector Anthony of Hull Police was cycling along Beverley High Road in the City. He was in uniform and was on his way to Norfolk Street station to finish his tour of duty. It had been the usual fairly routine late afternoon shift — Sundays in the year 1936 were pretty quiet after the mayhem which always broke out on Saturday nights. He noticed a young man standing on the footpath further down the road and as he drew nearer he recognised 25-year old Arthur Smith North, a boot repairer and son of his erstwhile colleague Inspector North who had died recently. The family lived in Belvoir Street.

To his surprise the young man signalled him to stop and dismounting from his cycle he smiled a greeting and said "What's up then?" "Read that," said a nervous looking North handing the Inspector a bank book. The Inspector had always privately considered Arthur to be a slightly 'strange' lad but was quite unprepared for what was written on the fly leaf of the book. "I have just killed a young woman" he read, "a girl I have been taking out two or three weeks lately — down Bentley bridlepath, on Beverley High Road. I am fed up with being off ill. I wanted to die and I took this course. I have nothing to say."

"Is this true?" asked the incredulous Inspector and when North nodded he took him to a nearby police box and started to question him. North claimed his victim was Elsa Meyer, his 17-year old friend from Francis Street, Hull and he said he had strangled her with his bare hands.

With other officers summoned by the Inspector now arriving, North was taken to the bridle path. Arrangements had been made to meet officers from the East Riding there because the crime would have taken place in their area.

As the party walked along they reached a field gate with a bunch of flowers tied to it. North said he had put the flowers there to mark the spot. In the field they found the body of a young fair haired woman covered with a coat. She was fully clothed and the body was still warm.

Superintendent Thompson from Beverley had by now joined the group and North was handed over to him and his officers. Taken back to Beverley and interrogated he eventually made a statement in which he alleged that the girl had promised to have sexual relations with him but when it came to the point she was not happy about it. She had said, "I don't want you but I don't want to let you down". North said he had lost his temper, put his hands around her throat and strangled her, finishing the job with a handkerchief. He went on, "I then tied the handkerchief round her throat tightly and left it for about quarter of an hour. She struggled a little at first and then lay quiet. I then took her coat which she had taken off when we came into the field and spread it over her. I walked up to the lane to the Beverley Road and while walking along I wrote my statement in my bank book."

North appeared before Magistrates at Beverley and after a lengthy hearing was committed for trial at York Assizes. The only evidence called for the Defence was the local doctor, Dr. Lavine who said the prisoner's health had been bad for some time and he thought this might make it more difficult for him to resist impulses which normal people could resist.

At the November Assizes in York, North appeared before Mr. Justice Goddard, later to become a Lord Chief Justice of England renowned for his stern attitude to criminals.

The story unfolded before the Jury with Mr. A. Morley KC and Mr. W. R. Lawrence appearing for the crown. Mr. R. Paley Scott KC represented North and called on Doctor Levine in evidence.

After the doctor had given his evidence, again citing his belief that North's medical condition made him subject to uncontrollable impulses Mr. Scott addressed the Jury. "If the law says in these circumstances a man is responsible, so be it. The law must be carried out. But I ask you to believe that this young man was acting at the time under some impulse for which he was not responsible." No sooner had he uttered these words than Mr. Justice Goddard interrupted. "I cannot accept that in support of a plea of insanity Mr. Scott. It has been held over and over again that an irresistible impulse is no excuse."

It took only half-an-hour for the Jury to reach a verdict. North collapsed in the dock as the foreman said, "Guilty" and the Judge donned the black cap and said, "The Jury have found you guilty of the murder of Miss Meyer and I have no wish to add to the pains you must now be suffering but I will simply pronounce the sentence it is my duty to pronounce." North was carried below, a condemned man!

He was moved to Hull prison and placed in the condemned cell with two warders permanently present. The execution was fixed for 9.0 am on 30th January. As this was unusual with executions usually being at 8.0 am before normal prison routine begins the Prison Commissioners wrote to the Governor.

"As this execution is to take place at 9.0 am the Commissioners request you to arrange that the usual prison routine should be followed during the time of the execution so that the prisoners would be scattered over the prison at their respective tasks; their minds would be occupied; any noise from the trap door would pass unnoticed. Suggest early morning exercise as usual, work commenced 8.30 am. Prisoners normally employed near the execution shed should be given extra exercise remote from it. The prison clock chime to be disconnected before 9.0 am. Executioners to be lodged so that they neither enter the prison or cross the yards."

A terrified North was carefully watched by his ever present escort. His Appeal was heard on 14th December when Mr. Paley Scott argued that the trial Judge had misdirected the Jury on the question of insanity and he explained how North had marked the murder scene with flowers and had murdered the girl and given himself up rather than commit suicide.

Rejecting the appeal the Lord Chief Justice of England said, "It is interesting how often the defence of insanity is put forward when punishment for the crime is death but seldom if ever in other cases!"

Christmas was fast approaching and the plight of Arthur Smith North caught the imagination of the folk in Hull. A stand was set up on Monument Bridge for people to sign a petition for a reprieve and long queues waiting to add their names.

An enormous petition was eventually forwarded to Home Office where the usual procedures, when an execution was

THE DAILY MAIL, TUESDAY, NOVEMBER 17, 1936.

PETITION FOR CONDEMNED HULL YOUTH
HIS STEPMOTHER'S TEARS

imminent, had been moving smoothly into action. The opinion of the trial Judge was sought and precedents checked.

On Christmas Eve the Home secretary annouced he would recommend the new King George VI to use his perogative for the first time to reprieve a condemned man. Arthur Smith North's sentence was commuted to Life Imprisonment.

He became a model prisoner and was released quietly back into the community from Camp Hill Prison, Isle of Wight on 24th November 1943, having served between 7 and 8 years.

THE MAN WHO WANTED TO HANG

The City of Kingston-upon-Hull lay badly bruised but unbowed as it sprawled along the northern bank of the Humber estuary just after the second World War had come to an end. Despite suffering heavy air raids the great sea port throbbed with the life which is associated with centres of commerce. Not only were many and varied cargoes entering and leaving the port it was also home to one of the world's greatest fishing fleets, still sailing fearlessly into distant waters despite all the enemy and the weather could throw their way.

Alongside with the prosperity brought by a thriving commercial life the city had a sleazy side where drunkenness, prostitution and crime generally flourished.

A 29-year old Scotsman James Inglis was typical of the human flotsam which got washed up in all cities but particularly those which were ports. Initially arriving in Hull in the army he had been discharged to De la Pole mental hospital on the outskirts. Released from there just before Christmas 1945 and attracted by the bright lights he had moved into the city centre and found lodgings in a terraced house in Barmston Street in the east of the city.

Landlord Herbert Bell and his common-law wife Amy Gray took him in despite knowing he had been committed to a mental hospital for attacking a woman. They said afterwards he was such an insignificant, quiet and inoffensive individual they felt sure he would be no trouble. It hadn't been easy to obtain lodgers and they had needed the extra money.

Inglis joined the easily recognisable group of people who float round the edge of society in large cities. Workshy he had lots of odd jobs which he usually kept for days only before being either dismissed or leaving of his own accord. His diet consisted largely of fish and chips and his only desire was to hang around seeking drink and women in the low class pubs. He lived largely on his wits.

Alice Morgan on the other hand had been one of a well respected Hull family, her father was a trawler captain and she married a wealthy money lender by whom she had two children before

BARMSTON ST

getting divorced. Her life then slipped rapidly down hill and she soon resorted to prostitution to earn a living. Although 50-years old she retained a slim and shapely figure and was very attractive to the men who sought her services. Also, despite her work she was a very friendly soul always willing to help anyone in need.

How she and Inglis first met is not clear but he started going to her house in Cambridge Street and paying for sex. Before long they were seen more and more together and while Alice treated the relationship as a purely business one, Inglis was deceived by her friendliness into thinking he meant something special to her. He began to think of her as his girlfriend.

To the city of Hull at the time they were two inconsequential lives until they suddenly hit the headlines in February 1946.

Inglis had been working at a Hessle shipyard and, true to form, had given a 'minute's notice' and walked out. He said he had decided to return to his home in Scotland. After going to Barmston Street and changing into his best suit he returned to Hessle for his outstanding wages.

With just over £5 weighing down his pockets, instead of leaving for the north he went into the city centre for a drink. One became two and.... he stayed until he was kicked out at closing time in the afternoon and wandered round until he met Alice. She agreed they should go back to her home and he suggested they get some drink. She went to the Victoria Vaults but they refused to serve her because they had closed.

By 6.0 pm they were waiting impatiently for the landlord at the Queen's Head to open in Walker Street and as they were his only customers that early he listened as Inglis spoke about going back into the Foreign Legion. After a short while the pair left and made their way to the Victoria Vaults and here Alice had a conversation with her long time friend Hannah Short.

At 8 o'clock Inglis suggested they went back to Cambridge Street and Alice agreed but when they arrived they had a furious row,

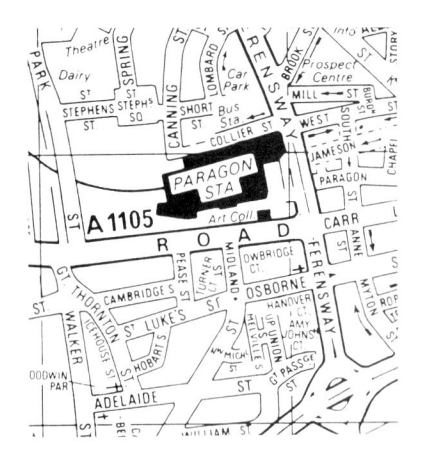

Inglis wanted intercourse and Alice refused unless he paid. Imagining their relationship had developed past such commercialism and having no money anyway, Inglis insisted and Alice resisted. Things got more and more heated and when she taunted him that she knew a chap who would pay her £5 to go with her that evening the Scotsman's temper snapped. He struck her, knocked her down and then carried on hitting her with a savage ferocity quite amazing for a person of his size and physique. Blood flew everywhere and he turned his attention to smashing the furniture as his raging continued. Alice Morgan was an inert heap and after looking at her dispassionately for a few minutes Inglis casually hunted around until he found a crowbar and forced the gas meter for the few shillings it contained before leaving the house.

About an hour later Hannah Short, still in the Vaults, saw Inglis come in. She noticed nothing unusual about him and when she asked where Alice was he said she had gone to bed feeling unwell. After a few minutes he went quietly on his way.

Similarly neither Herbert Bell nor Amy Gray noticed anything unusual when Inglis reached his lodgings. Discovering he had not eaten, the motherly Amy went out and brought him fish and chips. He ate it quietly and went to bed but could not sleep with Alice's body haunting his mind.

It was 36 hours before an errand boy calling at Alice's house failed to get a reply and pushed open the unlocked door and tiptoed into the sitting room. The curtains were drawn and seeing the dark figure on the couch he assumed she was asleep and crept out again.

At about the same time Inglis went back to his lodgings where Amy was on her own. She, worried about his rent, started to question him about work and the rent. Inglis seemed confused and unable to speak coherently which worried Amy further and she persisted with her questioning. Eventually he mumbled she should go to his room and look in his box for money. As she was bending over the box blows rained on the back of her head and suddenly she was being strangled from behind. She slumped to the ground, her consciousness gone and Inglis ran from the house assuming he had killed her.

On the Saturday postman Harry Thomas tried to deliver a registered letter to Alice Morgan and, receiving no reply he returned at noon. Again unsuccessful he contacted a neighbour and she went into the house only to flee in fright when she saw the dark bundle on the couch. Thomas tried to waken the figure and when he raised the cover he saw the smashed, bloody face. It was so battered he mistook it for a man.

Police were informed and it wasn't long before Chief Constable Sidney Lawrence and Detective Inspector Jim Cocksworth were at the scene. When they came to examine the body the injuries were horrific. Naked from the waist down, a silk stocking used as a ligature was deeply embedded in the skin of the throat. The tongue was stuck out of the mouth like a balloon and was later found to be pierced by five teeth. Almost all the facial bones had been pulverised and even the hardened police surgeon blanched at the thought of the violence involved.

While the Chief Constable was blandly misleading the press by telling them there was no idea who the attacker was, Cocksworth was already hunting for Inglis. He already knew about the attack on Amy Gray because she had miraculously survived and managed to crawl downstairs into the street where she was found. Rumours rapidly circulated in the city and both police and public were terrified the maniac might strike again.

Buses, trains and even ferries were checked and watched, the city was flooded with police and every bar and club was visited. As shops closed and Saturday evening crowds built up police scanned faces for the wanted man. It was not until 11.0 pm that Inglis was found. He had been found cowering in a room in the Salvation Army hostel in Great Passage Street. Far from being a raving maniac he turned out to be a pathetically cowering and whimpering creature dying to confess his crime.

"I knew you'd be coming — you know Cambridge Street — I done it — I killed a woman." he blurted out as soon as Cocksworth identified himself. When the Inspector started to tell him what he was suspected of Inglis broke in and pleaded, "Don't tell me anymore about it please sir, I've been walking ever since and I'm glad you've come!"

Told he was being arrested the Scotsman said, "Yes I know, I went barmy. Please don't tell me anymore about it — I did it".

A detective constable was detailed to guard him while arrangements were made to take him to the police station and when they were alone Inglis suddenly said, "You'd better go to Barmston Street as well. There's another one there, I went barmy there too." The detective said, "I must tell you that you are not obliged to say anything unless ...." Inglis cut in, "Is she dead?" When told Amy had survived Inglis said, "Thank God, I thought there was two".

Tried and convicted at Leeds Assizes Mr. Justice Gorman paused before sentence to ask the prisoner if he had anything to say before sentence was passed. An audible gasp arose from the spectators when Inglis blurted, "I've had a fair trial from you and members of your court. All I ask is that you get me hanged as soon as possible!"

He declined to appeal and his execution was fixed for May 8th at Strangeways prison Manchester. Here Syd Dearnley, assistant to Albert Pierrepoint, executioner at the time, takes up the tale. Arriving at the prison the day prior to the execution the two hangmen observed Inglis through a special spy hole in his cell door to assess his build and weight to ensure they planned the correct length of drop. They were surprised to see the condemned man playing cards and laughing and joking with his warders. Next morning arrangements were completed early in the execution chamber which as usual was next to the condemned cell. The assistant executioner recalled that 'we walked into the condemned cell on the stroke of the hour. As we entered Inglis turned round and looked at us. Then he started to smile! At first it was little more than a twitch of his mouth muscles but blossoming quickly into a full smile as if he were pleased to see us!

As if that was not enough, he then turned his back on us and brought his arms up behind him, hands crossed. He was trying to assist us! As we reached him, I gently took hold of his right arm and raised it slightly. He was being so bloody helpful he was getting in the way! An instant later Pierrepoint was ready for the arm and I lowered it into his grip.

Without any prompting from me, Inglis now turned and saw the rope waiting for him through the double doors. He smiled again and started towards it. He was about to lead us into the execution chamber!

It must have been a hell of a shock for Pierrepoint. He recovered and managed to get in front, but as he shot past, Inglis speeded up. The man was almost treading on Pierrepoint's heels in his anxiety to get on to the gallows. Pierrepoint looked over his shoulder and started trotting. The two screws who were there to help us fell behind as I hurried after them!

We literally trotted into the execution chamber. (Pierrepoint was trotting to stay ahead of Inglis, he was trotting to get there as quickly as he could and I was trotting to keep up with everybody!). As we arrived on the drop I just had time to register the open-mouthed astonishment of someone in the official party before I bent down to strap the legs. Then Inglis was away on that long eight-foot drop before I had properly stood up again.

The whole thing had been quite incredible, so fast it was unbelievable. I went down in the pit a few minutes later as the doctor checked the corpse, when I heard someone up above saying, with disbelief in his voice, "Seven seconds, it took seven seconds!"'

Albert Pierrepoint was later to claim that this hanging was the quickest there had ever been, a truly macabre way for the nonentity that was James Inglis to make his mark in the history of our criminal justice system.

MURDER IN YORK

Outwardly all was calm on a crisp winter's night in January 1951 in the quiet little housing estate in York. Inside the comfortable house of retired joiner Walter Wylde however, things were anything but calm. His voice raised in anger, the 72-year old Walter argued vigorously with his visitor. The replies were quieter but increasingly filled with menace. A knife was produced and within seconds the pensioner was fighting for his life. Fit for his age and determined, so great were his efforts not to succumb that he was later found to have burst his arm muscles. But he was no match for his assailant and despite all his efforts resulting in multiple cuts and slashes on his arms and hands, eventually he collapsed — the knife had pierced his chest and entered his heart.

Comfortably off, Walter and his wife had retired from Halifax in West Yorkshire to York after the end of the Second World War. His wife had died in 1949 but Walter had kept himself busy and had taken the precaution of telling his neighbour, Mrs. Raby, that if she ever failed to see him about in a morning she was to investigate in case he was ill.

Mrs. Raby didn't see him on Sunday 28th January and went to the house and found it locked and secured. Peering through the window she could just see what looked like a body on the kitchen floor. She immediately called the York Police.

Detective Inspector Ernest Wild, head of York C.I.D. was called to the scene and was soon joined by the City's Chief Constable, Mr. Herman. There was no sign of any forced entry into the house where the body had been found so it was immediately assumed the attacker could have been known to his victim. Initial enquiries in the area and with people who knew Walter gave no clue as to a possible suspect. He had been playing whist at York Rugby League club during the evening prior to his body being found.

Aware of the limited experience of officers in his small force, Mr. Herman immediately considered asking for assistance from the Murder Squad at Scotland Yard. He knew that if he asked Home Office for such help within 72 hours of a murder being discovered no charges would be made for the service. Feeling he had nothing to lose he made his request and Detective Superintendent Jack Capstick and a sergeant from C.1.Department at Scotland Yard were immediately despatched by train to York.

After being briefed the two Yard men immediately set about organising enquiries using a system pioneered over years by the Metropolitan police. House to house enquiries were gradually extended over a wide area and enquiries were made with all persons who could be traced, who had had any connections whatsoever with Walter and his wife. Every person interviewed either completed a questionnaire or made a witness statement. Every detail recorded was indexed and cross indexed and checked back at the Murder Room. Capstick had an enviable reputation in the nation which he was keen to maintain.

155 Huntingon Road. Scene of Walter Wylde's murder.

A particular difficulty with the York case was establishing a motive. There had been no break-in, money and jewellery in the house had not been touched. Walter had no known enemies or dubious associates.

However, the system paid off when Scotsman John Dand was interviewed as someone who had known the Wyldes. An ex desert rat he and his family had for some years been neighbours of the Wyldes until moving back to Scotland. Shortage of work had brought Dand back to York a month before the murder and he had moved into lodgings in the city. Routinely asked to account for his movements on the Saturday evening/Sunday morning of the murder he had claimed he was drinking in the sergeants' mess at Strensall Barracks until 8.15 pm. He had then had drinks in a few public houses and was talking to old army mates, who he named, until about 10.45 pm. Medical evidence had put the time of death before 10.0 pm.

When his story was checked one of the sergeants he had been talking to disputed the time Dand had left them. He said it had been much earlier!

Capstick realised that here was someone who had to be treated as a suspect until proved otherwise. He instructed a small team to visit and search Dand's lodgings. This was done and his landlady remembered he had not returned home until 11.30 pm on the Saturday night. His room revealed a quantity of clothing which was bloodstained and, more significantly, a letter from Dand's wife in Scotland enclosing two from Walter Wyldes. Apparently Dand had borrowed small sums of money from Walter when they were neighbours — £3 for a pair of overalls and another sum of £3. Walter complained in the letter that he had only been repaid one of the sums and asked if the outstanding money could be forwarded so that he could pay his rates.

Scenting a good lead police arrested Dand and he was taken to York police headquarters where he was interviewed by Capstick. When asked where the blood on his clothes had come from he claimed he had been with a prostitute after leaving his friends on Saturday and when he got home he discovered the blood.

Remanded in custody for seven days Dand was a very subdued man when he was next interviewed by Capstick who told him the blood on his suit was Group 'A' — Walter Wyldes' group. His own blood was Group 'O'. Within a short time he confessed and said he had gone to see Walter about the money and they had rowed about it.

Charged with murder by Inspector Wild the 33-years old Dand was committed for trial at Leeds Assizes. Here he pleaded not guilty and retracted his confession. Found guilty he was sentenced to death and his appeal was dismissed by the Court of Criminal Appeal.

John Dand was hanged at Strangeways Prison, Manchester on 12th June 1951 and as so often happens, two men had died over a paltry sum of money.

MURDER IN THE DESERT

Widowed Elizabeth Houghton who lived at 5 Stirling Terrace, Ripon Street, East Hull was proud of her son Tom. After doing his national service in the Royal Army Service Corps and taking a liking to the life he had signed on as a regular soldier.

Quiet and competent in his work as an army storeman he was popular with his fellow soldiers and in December 1949 he was posted to the Canal Zone at Suez.

Working on the military base was a local Egyptian girl 20-year old Iro Hadjifoti who was single and at the later trial became known as 'the Girl in Blue'. Houghton was to claim Iro had agreed to marry him although no evidence could be found that he had ever had an association with her.

There is little doubt that the young Corporal, who was also single, developed a fascination for the beautiful Egyptian which resulted in him fantasysing that she was his girl friend. At some stage Houghton began pestering the girl and his unit commander, Captain Mason, warned him to leave her alone. There is little doubt that Houghton decided, rightly or wrongly, that the warning was given because the Captain had designs on the girl himself.

In February 1952 a Unit birthday party was being celebrated in the Canteen and officers and men, families and friends were having a jolly time. Mason himself had been drinking elsewhere during the day but according to friends was not drunk. He walked past the outside of the canteen where the party was going on and, looking through the window, saw Iro and Captain Mason dancing together. Consumed with an overpowering sense of jealousy Tom Houghton went back to his barracks and collected his Sten Gun, a weapon capable of devastating bursts of automatic fire at short range.

Walking to the canteen he entered the crowded room and was heard to be muttering, "I want Mason!" He approached the unsuspecting officer and without warning opened fire. There were screams and uproar ensued as men present went to disarm him. Captain Mason lay dead on the floor.

HULL N.C.O. FACES MURDER CHARGE
'RAN AMOK WITH STEN GUN'
—SAY PROSECUTION

Houghton was arrested and charged with murder and confined in the British Military Prison in the desert at Fanara, between Fayid and Suez.

As the offence was by a British serviceman on a fellow serviceman in a foreign country, the matter would be dealt with by a military Court Martial. Lt. Col. McCullock was deputed to be the Prosecuting Officer and Mr. Percy Grieve, a Barrister was flown out from England to undertake the defence.

At the trial the defence could do little except to try and mitigate the seriousness of the charge and they tried to persuade the Court that Houghton had been insane at the time, the insanity brought about by his compulsive infatuation with the girl Iro.

The hearing was over in a day and the Court took a mere 47 minutes to find Tom Houghton guilty of murder. The Brigadier who was President of the Court rose gravely to his feet and as the soldier stood stiffly to attention in front of him, he sentenced him to death by hanging.

Returned to his little white walled cell at Fanara, Tom Houghton was to wait here with windows barred and only his guards as company for the next three months. An appeal was launched and rejected and the sentence was then sent for review by Lt. General Sir John Erskine, Commander of the Canal Zone and then by the Middle East Commander in Chief General Sir Brian Robertson. Neither could find any reason to interfere with the sentence.

Meanwhile back in Hull the pathetic plight of his widowed mother was felt by the whole City. A massive petition was raised and forwarded to the Authorities begging for mercy and Commander H. Pursey, M.P. for East Hull arranged for Mrs. Houghton to be flown at public expense to see her son.

Learning that the petition for a reprieve had been rejected, Mrs. Houghton set off for Egypt from RAF Lyneham at 6.0 am on 21st June 1952. The execution of her son was fixed for dawn on the 24th.

The prison authorities felt great sympathy for the lonely woman who had travelled so far to see a son she had not seen for two years and who was now condemned to die. They allowed the two to stay together for as long as possible.

Next day, on Tuesday 24th June 1952 and while his mother's plane was grounded by engine trouble in Malta, Corporal Thomas Houghton from Hull was hanged in the desert of North Africa by Albert Pierrepoint, Britain's official executioner. Only two other people were present at his end — the Chaplain and the Assistant Provost Marshall.

CANTEEN PARTY MURDERER

HOUGHTON HANGED AT DAWN

AN ETERNAL TRIANGLE AT HESSLE

It was 1.15 am on Friday 19th of October 1962 when Roy Bigby, small holder and a partner in a boarding kennel business returned to his premises Fullstryde Kennels, Hessle because he was worried about the activities of vandals. He had been to Hull Fair with a group of friends which included Marjorie Hutchinson the 42-years old wife of his partner in the dog business — Leslie Hutchinson. Reaching the track leading to the kennels he was surprised to see Leslie Hutchinson's motor cycle lying on its side. He also saw an injured man laying a little further up the road.

Without further ado he rushed to the nearest telephone but finding it damaged and out of order he walked to Hessle police station to report the incident. Police and ambulance crews who attended what had sounded like a road accident found, to their surprise, the dead body of Leslie Hutchinson. His injuries had obviously been the result of a vicious attack and he had been battered about the head and strangled with a belt from his own trousers. Only 5'7" but a stocky and very strong ships' welder the murdered man had obviously put up a determined struggle. Blood was everywhere.

Superintendents Bennett and Boam and Detective Chief Inspector Eric Tiplady of the East Riding Constabulary took charge of enquiries but only a day had passed before Chief Constable Blenkin decided to call in assistance from the murder squad at Scotland Yard. Detective Superintendent John Bailey and Detective Sergeant Fyall travelled from London to lead the investigation.

It transpired Mrs. Hutchinson had gone to Hull Fair with Bigby and a group of friends during the evening prior to the murder, leaving the deceased who disliked fairs doing a number of odd jobs. Police enquiries were intense with a number of major searches for the murder weapon carried out by sixty East Riding men supported by officers from Hull. Forensic Scientists were called in and house to house visits made in the area.

Initially interest was centred on a report that a long distance lorry driver had picked a man up on the A63 road near Hessle on the night in question. The man had been covered in blood and said he had been in an accident. Widespread enquiries were made in the north London area where the man had been dropped, with no result. Newspapers confirmed that both Mrs. Hutchinson and Roy Bigby were doing their best to assist in the enquiry.

A fortnight passed and public interest in the crime was just beginning to wane when the dramatic news broke that Marjorie Hutchinson, Roy Bigby and a meat porter — Frederick Green had been arrested and charged jointly with murder!

The full story did not emerge until the committal proceedings before magistrates sitting at Beverley Sessions House on 15th and 17th December. It was claimed Mrs. Hutchinson had started an affair with Bigby and was determined to get rid of her husband so that not only would she be free to go with Bigby but would also inherit some money from her husband's insurance. She encouraged Bigby to find someone willing to murder Hutchinson and he located the 34-years old Green who agreed to help in return for any money on the victim's body.

Together, Green and Bigby set a trap for Hutchinson on the evening of the murder and stretched a chest high wire across the track leading to the kennels. When their unsuspecting victim rode up on his motor cycle he was unseated by the wire and set upon by Green and Bigby. After the struggle Green's hands were covered with blood. Bigby then went on to meet Mrs. Hutchinson and together they went to the fair, returning later to casually report the alleged finding of the body.

The three accused appeared at Leeds Assizes in January 1963 and Hutchinson and Bigby pleaded not guilty while Green admitted the crime. His attitude allowed the prosecution to have him dealt with and then produce him as a witness to give his damning evidence against the other two. Eventually Hutchinson and Bigby were found guilty and she was sentenced to life imprisonment. Green also received a life sentence while Bigby was found not guilty of murder but guilty of conspiring to assault and beat the dead man and he was sentenced to three years imprisonment.

EPILOGUE

This book has only covered a very tiny proportion of the executions which have taken place in this small part of the country, over the years. All the more modern cases involved homicide. The lives of the victims were threatened and in most of the cases ended. Ended by other humans who ranged from viciously callous, through temporarily deranged to the woefully inadequate.

The deaths of those murdered were dreadful tragedies but so in their way were the macabre rituals which had to be undergone by the condemned. From the donning of the black cap to pass sentence; the weeks of unbelievable suspense in the condemned cell with life hanging on the whim of the Home Secretary; to the final act of being hanged by the neck until dead!

Originally those to be executed stood at the gallows on a sledge or cart which was pulled from under them allowing the rope to strangle the person. Trap doors came into use before the end of public executions and in all hanging cases the length of the drop became critical in ensuring a speedy death. In the early public executions with trap doors, if the hangman miscalculated they were known to expedite matters by putting their own weight on the condemned person, often helped by willing spectators, to finish the job!

The same ghoulish, compulsive curiosity which made a man collect bloodstained sand from the murder scene on a Withernsea beach also ensured crowds at public executions. Even when executions were moved behind the closed doors of prisons crowds still gathered outside at the appointed hour.

Whether the fear and horror of being executed ever entered the minds of murderers or acted as a deterrent to any is doubtful. The numbers of homicides in England and Wales has shown little significant change since the abolition of the death penalty. The wise Lord Denning once said, "It is a mistake to look on the object of punishment as being deterrent, reformative, preventative or anything else. The ultimate justification of punishment is not that of a deterrent but is the emphatic denunciation by the community,

The six steps which used to be taken by persons on their way to execution at Hull prison. The wall on the right shows new brickwork which was originally the door to the execution chamber. A door which is set back to the left of figure 13 on the photograph, was the entrance to the condemned cell.

of a crime." In fact some terrorist murderers whose crime is political would welcome death as a chance for martyrdom.

There are some horrible murders which in public opinion still justify the death penalty and there is a strong lobby for the return of the hangman. But an execution is a very final act and many people who have recently been judged to have been wrongly convicted of murder would have received posthumous pardons, not freedom and life!

Timothy Evans was wrongly hanged for a crime committed by John Christie — how many others have been the subject of such bizarre and terrible judicial mistakes?

The writer of this book was involved in one of the last murder cases where the culprit was hanged. It was after the 1957 Homicide Act decreed only certain types of murder should be capital offences. The man, George Riley, a 21-year old butcher from Shrewsbury, was convicted of murdering an elderly neighbour "in the furtherance of theft". He was convicted mainly upon his statement of admission to police. In that statement five words! five small words meant the difference between George Riley living or dying! Those words were "I went in to steal". Most of those involved in the case which attracted massive national publicity, felt uneasy after George died! It is an unease that never goes away.

Only one set of working gallows exists in England today — at Pentonville Prison in London. Only three crimes still carry the death penalty — Treason; Piracy on the high seas; and Arson in the Royal Dockyards! It is unlikely that anyone will ever again have to walk the dreadful six steps from condemned cell to execution shed in this country. A very good riddance to the overworked and groaning Gallows!